Marx
Joyce
Abbott Hardy Machiavelli Chesterton Cooper Emerson Austen
Defoe Melville Montaigne Haggard Hugo Grimm
Carroll Christie Eliot
Stoker Molière
Wilde Maupassant Byron Schiller
Garnett Einstein Fitzgerald Engels Smith Kafka
Goethe Hawthorne Hall
Cotton Dostoyevsky Willis
Baum Henry Kipling Doyle
Leslie Dumas Flaubert Turgenev Nietzsche Balzac
Stockton Vatsyayana Crane
Burroughs Verne
Curtis Tocqueville Gogol Vinci
Homer Widger Tolstoy Whitman Busch
Darwin Thoreau
Potter Freud Zola Lawrence Twain Scott Plato Harte
Kant Jowett Stevenson Dickens Burton Hesse
Andersen
London Descartes Cervantes Voltaire
Poe Aristotle Wells Burton Cooke
Hale James Hastings
Bunner Shakespeare Irving
Richter Chambers
Doré Chekhov Benedict Alcott
Dante Shaw Pushkin
Swift Wodehouse Newton

 tredition®

tredition was established in 2006 by Sandra Latusseck and Soenke Schulz. Based in Hamburg, Germany, tredition offers publishing solutions to authors and publishing houses, combined with worldwide distribution of printed and digital book content. tredition is uniquely positioned to enable authors and publishing houses to create books on their own terms and without conventional manufacturing risks.

For more information please visit: www.tredition.com

TREDITION CLASSICS

This book is part of the TREDITION CLASSICS series. The creators of this series are united by passion for literature and driven by the intention of making all public domain books available in printed format again - worldwide. Most TREDITION CLASSICS titles have been out of print and off the bookstore shelves for decades. At tredition we believe that a great book never goes out of style and that its value is eternal. Several mostly non-profit literature projects provide content to tredition. To support their good work, tredition donates a portion of the proceeds from each sold copy. As a reader of a TREDITION CLASSICS book, you support our mission to save many of the amazing works of world literature from oblivion. See all available books at www.tredition.com.

Project Gutenberg

The content for this book has been graciously provided by Project Gutenberg. Project Gutenberg is a non-profit organization founded by Michael Hart in 1971 at the University of Illinois. The mission of Project Gutenberg is simple: To encourage the creation and distribution of eBooks. Project Gutenberg is the first and largest collection of public domain eBooks.

An Essay on the Lyric Poetry of the Ancients

John Ogilvie

Imprint

This book is part of TREDITION CLASSICS

Author: John Ogilvie
Cover design: Buchgut, Berlin – Germany

Publisher: tredition GmbH, Hamburg - Germany
ISBN: 978-3-8472-1420-5

www.tredition.com
www.tredition.de

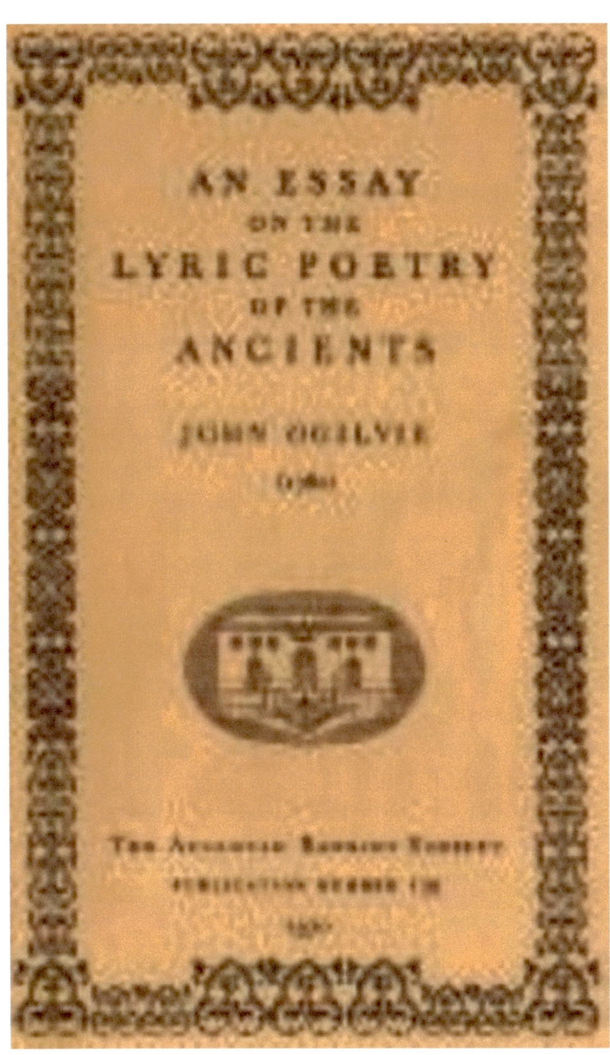

AN ESSAY
ON THE
LYRIC POETRY
OF THE
ANCIENTS

JOHN OGILVIE
(1762)

THE AUGUSTAN REPRINT SOCIETY
PUBLICATION NUMBER 139
1970

THE AUGUSTAN REPRINT SOCIETY

JOHN OGILVIE

AN

ESSAY

ON THE

LYRIC POETRY

OF THE

ANCIENTS

(1762)

Introduction by
WALLACE JACKSON

PUBLICATION NUMBER 139
WILLIAM ANDREWS CLARK MEMORIAL LIBRARY
UNIVERSITY OF CALIFORNIA, LOS ANGELES

1970

i

INTRODUCTION

John Ogilvie (1733-1813), Presbyterian divine and author, was one of a group of Scottish literary clergy and a fellow of the Edinburgh Royal Society. Chambers and Thomson print the following generous estimation of his work:

> Of all his books, there is not one which, as a whole, can be expected to please the general reader. Noble sentiments, brilliant conceptions, and poetic graces, may be culled in profusion from the mass; but there is no one production in which they so predominate, (if we except some of the minor pieces,) as to induce it to be selected for a happier fate than the rest. Had the same talent which Ogilvie threw away on a number of objects, been concentrated on one, and that one chosen with judgment and taste, he might have rivalled in popularity the most renowned of his contemporaries.1

The present letters reproduced here, along with the two volumes of his *Philosophical and Critical Observations on Composition* (London, 1774), are Ogilvie's major contributions to literary criticism. The remainder of his work, which is extensive, is divided almost equally between poetry and theological inquiry. At least one of his poems, "The Day of Judgment" (1758), was known to Churchill, Boswell, and Johnson, but unfortunately for Ogilvie's reputation Johnson "saw nothing" in it.2

I shall attempt no special pleading for Ogilvie here; he is and shall remain a minor neoclassic theorist. At the very least, however, it can be said that his methods are reasonably various and that, while his general critical assumptions are not unique, his control is strong. The fluidity with which he moves from one related position to another indicates a mind well informed by the critical tenets of his own time. If he does not surprise, he is nevertheless an interesting and worthy exemplar of the ii psychological tradition in later eighteenth-century criticism; and his historicism provides, and is intended to provide, an extensive field for the workings of psychological inquiry.

Thus his initial inquiry, in the first letter, into the Aristotelian principles of imitation and harmony establishes each as "natural" to the mind, and his distinctions between the separate provinces of reason and imagination are for the purpose of assigning to each its separate intellectual capacities. From these orderings follows his idea that poetry is of an earlier date than philosophy, the product of an irregular faculty, less governable than the reason and of swifter development. In turn, these assumptions lead into a form of historical primitivism in which the products of the first poets were "extemporary effusions," rudely imitative of pastoral scenes or celebratory of the divine being. Thus the first generic distinction Ogilvie makes is between pastoral poetry and lyric; the function of the former is to produce pleasure, the latter to raise admiration of the powers presiding over nature. As poetry is more natural to the young mind than philosophy, so is the end of pastoral poetry more easily achieved than that of the lyric. The difference resides essentially in Ogilvie's notion that the pastoral poet contemplates "external objects," while the lyric poet regards that which is not immediately available to the senses and consequently requires a more exuberant invention. What follows upon these reflections is a rather ingenious form of historical progressivism in which the civilizing powers of the poet provide the principal justification for lyric poetry. At work in Ogilvie's thought is a conception of the mythopoeic function of the earliest poets whose names have come down to us. Such poets, however, did not create their mythos, but imbibed it from the earlier Egyptian civilization and formed disguised allegorical poems. Here the instructive function of the first poets is related to the enlarging of the reader's imagination, so that Ogilvie's rather shrewd defense of lyric poetry is based upon the civilizing effects of imaginative appeal.

The infancy of poetry is related to the infancy of civilization, and the analogical possibilities of the one to the other sustain his argument at every point. If his historicism is dubious, his discourse is neatly illustrative of a neoclassic critical method and of the kind of psychological assumptions upon iii which such arguments could proceed. From the rather copious use of allegory and metaphor, as civilizing instruments, Ogilvie traces the rise of the religious fable as part of the inevitable sequence of imaginative development. To account, therefore, for the irregularity of the ode, for the "enthusiasm, obscurity and exuberance" (p.xxiv) which continue to characterize it, he refers to its anciently established character, a character not susceptible to amelioration by speculative rules. He allows, however, that both the "Epopee" (or epic) and the drama were gradually improved, and the informing principle of his historical progressivism is again patent.

The modifications of the ode are from the fictitious theology of Orpheus and Museus to the elegance and grace of Anacreon, Horace, and Sappho. It is mainly Horace whom Ogilvie has in view as the exemplar of the lyric poet, though "a professed imitator both of Anacreon and Pindar" (p.xxx). We can distinguish, therefore, several different criteria which contribute to Ogilvie's criticism: (1)a unity of sentiment consistent with a variety of emotions; (2)a propriety of the passions in which vivacity is controlled by the circumstances of character; (3)a just relation between language and sentiment; (4)elegant and pointed expression ("sallies and picturesque epithets" [p.xxxi.]) both to heighten the passions expressed and to draw from them their less obvious effects. Such distinctions define Ogilvie's typical insistence upon copying Nature, by which he means that the lyric poet's task is not only to follow the workings of the mind, but to heighten passion in a way that is more consistent with the nature of the passion itself than with its action in any particular mind. His criticism looks to the representation of "the internal movements of the mind warmed by imagination," yet "exposed in the happiest and most agreeable attitudes" (p.xxxv). The relation between the empirical and the ideal is a crux common to Ogilvie and neoclassic theory, not entirely resolved here by the practical and referential method of citing Horace's shorter odes. But it is a subject which comes in for more extended treatment in his second letter, in my judgment a far more critically ambitious letter and one in which his very fair critical abilities are more conspicuously apparent.

The second letter undertakes to explain the rules of lyric poetry, even as the first was concerned with the defects and iv causes of the poetry. Ogilvie rehearses a characteristic later eighteenth-century view of the imagination and makes again the conventional distinctions between faculties appropriate to philosophy and to poetry. His discussion of the function of judgment is, if anything, more conventional within the boundaries of neoclassic criticism than is his view of the imagination. Its typical role as concerned with the "disposition of materials" has a pedigree extending backward to Hobbes and the critical climate of the early years of Restoration England. Principally, Ogilvie is eager to assert that the poet is as judicious as the philosopher, by which, however, he does not intend to put forth a view of the cognitive function of the poet, but rather the justice with which he paints the passions. Essentially, therefore, Ogilvie's distinction between poet and philosopher is for the sake of distinguishing between the former's greater interest in the passions, the latter's more proper concern with the reason. Once again there is nothing unusual in his treatment of the subject at this time, with the possible exception that Ogilvie's conception of the imagination is not so comprehensive as that being developed by Alexander Gerard, William Duff, and some of the other contemporary associatioassociationistsnlsts. In order, however, to emphasize the importance of imagination, by which he largely means the imagistic liveliness of the poet's mind, he allows that the imagination is secondary only in didactic or ethical poetry. Such forms are perhaps best understood as hybrid, a kind of poetizing of philosophy, a sort of reasoning in verse, and therefore forms in which the imagination is not given full exercise. Given his premises it is not surprising that Ogilvie often emphasizes ornamentation or imagistic display and supports his position by conceiving of the modern lyric as descended from the religiously consecrated ode. The sublime and exuberant imagery of the latter exists reductively as an important virtue of the present lyric.

As Ogilvie develops his argument in the second letter, it is apparent also that the imagination functions as that faculty which best contemplates the sublime and the wonderful. The imagination is thus contemplative and expressive, and both functions are justified through the passions that admiration evokes. In sum, the imagination is evoked by the passions, a proposition which suggests why, for Ogilvie, the characteristic v mark of genius is a highly animated sensibility. It is apparent also that Ogilvie's criteria include sympathy, for sympathy is that which compels the transmission of the poet's sentiments to his readers. What is dimly present here is a theory of the poetic occasion, an occasion brought about by the poet's participation in a common cultural condition which inspires the communication of sentiments, both common and important, from one person to another. Corollary to this proposition is the notion that the poetic achievement is measured by the uniqueness of the poet's invention. Thus, it is not merely the poet's choice of a sublime subject that is important, but also the excellence with which he treats an unpromising subject. Ogilvie's criteria demand not merely a celerity of imagining, or a facility for the sublime, but a degree of innovativeness which wins the highest regard.

To follow the argument is to realize that his conception of the imagination includes judgment, celerity, and innovation. All three functions are basic to the imaginative act. It is the last, however, which he most emphasizes; and it is apparent, Ithink, that one intention of his argument is to refute the assumption that the sublime is the principal object of the poetic imagination. It is clear also that Ogilvie is attentive to the excesses of imagism, even as he makes the variety of a poet's images (along with the boldness of his transitions and the picturesque vivacity of his descriptions) one of the major terms of critical assessment. Especially, he is attentive to that which detracts from the principal object, and thus a kind of concentration of purpose emerges as a tacit poetic value, a concentration to which he refers as a "succession of sentiments which resemble ... the subject of his Poem" (lii). Here again Ogilvie has not so much a unity of structure in view as a unity of the passions, and it is this particular theme which generally guides his discourse; it is the general premise upon which his inquiry depends and on which his major justification of lyric poetry is based. In more modern terms we might here speak of the principle of the correlative, which Ogilvie rehearses in his treatment of the correspondence of subject and metaphor, and even indeed of metaphor as a mode of vision. Poetic discourse, for Ogilvie, does not depend upon metaphor, but without metaphor such discourse would be impossible.

vi

What is important, then, is the principle of propriety, a neat accord between the figure and the subject, a kind of aperçu. Thus, metaphors properly employed are "generally short, expressive, and

12

fitted to correspond with great accuracy to the point which requires to be illustrated" (pp.liii-liv). Second only to this consideration is that of color, by which he means tone or emphasis, and here again with a view toward the overall unity of the passions. It is perhaps worth noting that both considerations are relevant to Ogilvie's sense of the imagination as a judicious faculty operating independently of the reason, but nevertheless obedient to the laws of logical form, organic relationships, and proper successions, all of which imply an idea of structure.

Much of the time Ogilvie is occupied with quite familiar and conventional critical problems. The relation between regularity and irregularity is one that he particularly stresses, and his resolutions tend to allow a certain wildness as natural to the imagination, even as evidence of the faculty. He is, however, more inclined to permit bold and spirited transitions in the shorter ode than in the longer ode. As usual Ogilvie's critical principles are related to the nature of the work in question, and a greater irregularity is natural to the shorter ode since it presumes the imitation of the passions. But it is important to recognize that Ogilvie stresses not only the imitation of the passions, but the exercise of them as well; and the relation between the one and the other forms at bottom the larger principles on which his second letter is based. We might wish to say that he has in view the education of the passions, not merely by imitating them, but, as it were, by drawing from the reader his own possibilities for sensible response. It does not at all imply pre-romantic values to suggest that Ogilvie's criticism is directed toward a frank exploitation of the reader's emotion. As Maclean makes clear,3 such interests are hardly unique to romantic criticism. Bishop Lowth, for example, distinguished between the internal source and the external source of poetry, preferring the former because through it the mind is immediately conscious of itself and its own emotions.4 Ogilvie does not quite make the same statement, but his position easily coincides with it; and if, with John Crowe Ransom,5 we consider romantic poetry as uniquely directed toward the exploitation of the feelings, we shall be vii surprised by any number of minor eighteenth-century critics who are unabashedly interested in similar values. Ogilvie's position very much resembles Thomas Twining's view that the "description of passions and emotions by their sensible effects ... [is what] principally deserves the name of imitative."6

In accord with the psychological bias informing his essay, Ogilvie tends to reduce the importance of narrative events in favor of vivid and picturesque descriptions, for the latter most immediately communicate themselves to the reader and most expressly realize the translation from thought to feeling. Once again it is the uniqueness of rendering that he has in mind, the innovative cast of the poet's mind which transforms the familiar and by so doing gives it a newly affective power. It is important to recognize that Ogilvie shares with his contemporaries a more limited sense of the varieties of subject-matter than we are likely to grant. But as this is so for him, and as indeed this condition is a function of eighteenth-century historiography, it helps to explain the emphasis he places upon the uniqueness with which the subject is realized. Over and again such an interest shapes his inquiries and becomes both an attribute and a test of a poet's capacity. These remarks need to be qualified only by his inquiry into personification: for here it is the expectation of the mind that must not be disappointed, and that which is iconographically established (the figure of Time, for example) should not be violated.

While Ogilvie is not a major critic a good part of his charm and interest for us stems from a mind that is not in the least doctrinaire. His method is inductive, his appeal is always to the human psychology as that can be known experientially, and his standards are Aristotelian (if by such a reference we mean to signify a procedure based upon the known effects of known works). While there is nothing in these letters that deviates from the psychological tradition in later eighteenth-century criticism, it is also evident that Ogilvie is not really an associationist, and that he is less interested in the creative functioning of the poet's imagination than in the precepts of a psychological humanism which underscore his criteria and give validity to his remarks on the range and appeal of lyric poetry. In sum, his historicism exists as a justification for his defense of lyric poetry and is intended to provide a basis for the psychological bias of his argument.

Duke University

NOTES TO THE INTRODUCTION

1.*Biographical Dictionary of Eminent Scotsmen* (Glasgow, 1855), Vol. IV. For a list of Ogilvie's works consult Stephen and Lee, *Dictionary of National Biography* (Oxford, 1921-22), Vol. XIV. For an estimation of Ogilvie's relation to the theology of his own day consult James McCosh, *The Scottish Philosophy* (London, 1875).

2.*Life of Samuel Johnson*, ed. George Birkbeck Hill (Oxford, 1887), I., 421, 425.

3. Norman Maclean, "From Action to Image: Theories of the Lyric in the Eighteenth Century," in *Critics and Criticism Ancient and Modern*, ed. R.S. Crane (Chicago, 1952), pp. 408-463.

4. Ibid., p. 439.

5. John Crowe Ransom, *The New Criticism* (New York, 1941), p.15.

6.*An Inquiry into the Fine Arts* (London, 1784), p.6.

BIBLIOGRAPHICAL NOTE

This facsimile of *An Essay on the Lyric Poetry of the Ancients* (1762) is reproduced from a copy in the Duke University Library.

POEMS

ON

SEVERAL SUBJECTS.

TO WHICH IS PREFIX'D,

AN ESSAY

ON THE

LYRIC POETRY of the ANCIENTS;

In TWO LETTERS inscribed to

The Right Honourable JAMES Lord DESKFOORD. A

By *JOHN OGILVIE*, A.M.

LONDON:
Printed for G. KEITH, at the *Bible-and-Crown* in *Gracechurch-Street.*

M. DCC. LXII.

Although the facsimile includes this full Table of Contents, only the introductory section — the Essay on Lyric Poetry — was reprint-ed.

AN

ESSAY

ON THE

LYRIC POETRY

OF THE

ANCIENTS.

HUMBLY INSCRIBED

TO THE

RIGHT HONOURABLE

JAMES Lord DESKFOORD.
iiib2

AN

E S S A
Y

ON THE

LYRIC
POETRY
of the
ANCIENTS.

LETTER I.

MY LORD,

It is an observation, no doubt, familiar to your Lordship, that Genius is the offspring of Reason and Imagination properly moderated, and co-operating with united influence to promote the discovery, or the illustration of truth. Though it is certain that a separate province is assigned to each of these faculties, yet it often becomes a matter of the greatest difficulty to prevent them from making mutual encroachments, and from leading to extremes which are the more dangerous, because they are brought on by an imperceptible progression. iv — Reason in every mind is an uniform power, and its appearance is regular, and invariably permanent. When this Faculty therefore predominates in the sphere of composition, sentiments will follow each other in connected succession, the arguments employed to prove any point will be just and forcible; the stability of a work will be principally considered, and little regard will be payed to its exterior ornament. Such a work however, though it may be valued by a few for its intrinsic excellence, yet can never be productive of general improvement, as attention can only be fixed by entertainment, and entertainment is incompatible with unvaried uniformity1.

On the contrary, when Imagination is permitted to bestow the graces of ornament indiscriminately, we either find in the general that sentiments are superficial, and thinly scattered through a work, or we are obliged to search for them beneath a load of superfluous colouring. Such, my Lord, is the appearance of the superior Faculties of the mind when they are disunited from each other, or when either of them seems to be remarkably predominant.

Your Lordship is too well acquainted with this subject not to have observed, that in composition, as in common v life, extremes, however pernicious, are not always so distant from each other, as upon superficial inspection we may be apt to conclude. Thus in the latter, an obstinate adherence to particular opinions is contracted by observing the consequences of volatility; indifference ariseth from despising the softer feelings of tenderness; pride takes its origin from the disdain of compliance; and the first step to avarice is the desire of avoiding profusion. Inconveniencies similar to these are the consequences of temerity in canvassing the subjects of speculation. The mind of an Author receives an early bias from prepossession, and the dislike which he conceives to a particular fault precipitates him at once to the opposite extreme. For this reason perhaps it is, that young authors who possess some degree of Genius, affect on all occasions a florid manner2, and clothe their sentiments in the dress of imagery. To them nothing appears so disgusting as dry and lifeless uniformity; and instead of pursuing a middle course betwixt the extremes of profusion and sterility, they are only solicitous to shun that error of which Prejudice hath shown the most distorted resemblance. It is indeed but seldom, that Nature adjusts the intellectual balance so accurately as not to throw an *unequal weight* into either of the scales. vi Such likewise is the situation of man, that in the first stage of life the predominant Faculty engrosseth *his attention*, as the predominant Passion influenceth *his actions*. Instead therefore of strengthening the weaker power by assisting its exertions, and by supplying its defects, he is adding force to that which was originally too strong; and the same reflection which discovers *his error*, shows him likewise the difficulty of correcting it. Even in those minds, in which the distribution was primarily equal, education, habit, or some early bias is ready to break *that perfect poise* which is necessary to constitute consummate excellence.

From this account of the different manners, in which the faculties of the mind exert themselves in the sphere of competition, your Lordship will immediately observe, that the Poet who attempts to combine distant ideas, to catch remote allusions, to form vivid and agreeable pictures; is more apt from the very nature of his profession to set up a *false standard* of *excellence*, than the cool and dispassionate Philosopher who proceeds deliberately from position to argument, and who employs Imagination only as the Handmaid of a superior faculty. Having gone thus far, like persons who have got into a track from which they cannot recede, we may venture to proceed a step farther; and affirm that the *Lyric Poet* is exposed to this hazard more nearly than any other, and that to prevent vii him from falling into the extreme we have mentioned, will require the exercise of the closest attention.

That I may illustrate this observation as fully as the nature of the subject will permit, it will be expedient to enquire into the end which Lyric Poetry proposeth to obtain, and to examine the original standards from which the rules of this art are deduced.

Aristotle, who has treated of poetry at great length, assigns two causes of its origin,—*Imitation* and Harmony; both of which are natural to the human mind3. By Imitation he understands, "whatever employs means to represent any subject in a natural manner, whether it hath a real or imaginary existence4." The desire of imitating is originally stamped on the mind, and is a source of perpetual pleasure. "Thus" (says the great Critic) "though the figures of wild beasts, or of dead men, cannot be viewed as they naturally are without horror and reluctance; yet the Imitation of these in painting is highly agreeable, and our pleasure is augmented in proportion to that degree of resemblance which we conceive to subsist betwixt the Original and the Copy5." By Harmony he understands not the viii numbers or measures of poetry only, but that music of language, which when it is justly adapted to variety of sentiment or description, contributes most effectually to unite the pleasing with the instructive6. This indeed seems to be the opinion of all the Ancients who have written on this subject. Thus Plato says expressly, that those Authors who employ numbers and images without music have no other merit than that of throwing prose into measure7.

You will no doubt be of opinion, my Lord, upon reflecting on this subject, that Poetry was originally of an earlier date than Philosophy, and that its different species were brought to a certain pitch of perfection before that Science had been cultivated in an equal degree. Experience informs us on every occasion, that Imagination shoots forward to its full growth, and even becomes wild and luxuriant, when the reasoning Faculty is only beginning to open, and is wholly unfit to connect the series of accurate deduction. The information of the senses (from which Fancy generally borrows her images) always obtains the earliest credit, and makes for that reason the most lasting impressions. The sallies of this irregular Faculty ixc are likewise abrupt and instantaneous, as they are generally the effects of a sudden impulse which reason is not permitted to restrain. As therefore we have already seen, that the desire of imitating is *innate* to the mind (if your Lordship will permit me to make use of an unphilosophical epithet) and as the first inhabitants of the world were employed in the culture of the field, and in surveying the scenery of external Nature, it is probable that the first rude draughts of Poetry were extemporary effusions, either descriptive of the scenes of pastoral life, or extolling the attributes of the Supreme Being. On this account Plato says that Poetry was originally Ενθεος Μιμησις8, or an inspired imitation of those objects which produced either pleasure or admiration. To paint those objects which produced pleasure was the business of the pastoral, and to display those which raise admiration was the task consigned to the Lyric Poet. —To excite this passion, no method was so effectual as that of celebrating the perfections of the Powers who were supposed to preside over Nature. The Ode therefore in its first formation was a song in honour of these Powers9, either sung at solemn festivals or after the days of Amphion who was the inventor x of the Lyre, accompanied with the musick of that instrument. Thus Horace tellsus,

Musa dedit fidibus Divos, puerosque Divorum,10

The Muse to nobler subjects tun'd her lyre,

Gods, and the sons of Gods her song inspire. Francis.

In this infancy of the arts, when it was the business of the Muse, as the same Poet informsus,

Publica privatis secernere, sacra prophanis;

Concubitu prohibere vago, dare jura maritis,

Oppida moliri, leges includere ligno.11

Poetic Wisdom mark'd with happy mean,

Public and private, sacred and profane,

The wandering joys of lawless love supprest,

With equal rites the wedded couple blest,

Plann'd future towns, and instituted laws, &c. Francis.

your Lordship will immediately conclude that the species of Poetry which was first cultivated (especially when its end was to excite admiration) must for that reason have been the *loosest* and the most *undetermined.* There are indeed particular circumstances, by the concurrence of which one branch of an Art may be rendered perfect, when it is first introduced; and these circumstances were favourable to the Authors of the Eclogue. But whatever some readers may think, your Lordship will not look upon it as a paradox, to affirm that the same causes which produced xic2 this advantage to pastoral poetry, contributed in an equal degree to make the first Lyric Poems the most vague, uncertain, and disproportioncd standards.

In general it may be observed, that the difficulty of establishing rules is always augmented in proportion to the variety of objects which an Art includes. Pastoral Poetry is defined by an ingenious Author, to be an imitation of what may be supposed to pass among Shepherds12. This was accomplished the more easily by the first performers in this art, because they were themselves employed in the occupation which they describe, and the subjects which fell within their sphere must have been confined to a very narrow circle. They contented themfelves with painting in the simplest language the external beauties of nature, and with conveying an image of that age in which men generally lived on the footing of equality, and followed the dictates of an understanding uncultivated by Art. In succeeding ages, when manners became more polished, and the refinements of luxury were substituted in place of the simplicity of Nature, men were still fond of retaining an idea of this happy period (which perhaps originally existed in its full extent, only in the imagination of Poets) and the character of a perfect pastoral was xii justly drawn from the writings of those Authors who first attempted to excel in it13.

Though we must acknowledge, that the poetic representations of a *golden age* are chimerical, and that descriptions of this kind were not always measured by the standard of truth; yet it must be allowed at the same time, that at a period when Manners were uniform and natural, the Eclogue, whose principal excellence lies in exhibiting simple and lively pictures of common objects and common characters, was brought at once to a state of greater perfection by the persons who introduced it, than it could have arrived at in a more improved and enlightned aera.

You will observe, my Lord, that these circumstances were all of them unfavourable to Lyric Poetry. The Poet in this branch of his Art proposed as his principal aim to excite Admiration, and his mind without the assistance of critical skill was left to the unequal task of presenting succeeding ages with the rudiments of Science. He was at liberty indeed to range through the ideal world, and to collect images from every quarter; but in this research he proceeded without a guide, and his imagination xiii like a fiery courser with loose reins was left to pursue that path into which it deviated by accident, or was enticed by temptation. In short, Pastoral Poetry takes in only a few objects, and is characterized by that simplicity, tenderness, and delicacy which were happily and easily united in the work of an ancient Shepherd. He had little use for the rules of criticism, because he was not much exposed to the danger of infringing them. The Lyric Poet on the other hand took a more diversified and extensive range, and his imagination required a strong and steady rein to correct its vehemence, and restrain its rapidity. Though therefore we can conceive without difficulty, that the Shepherd in his poetic effusions might contemplate only the *external objects* which were presented to him, yet we cannot so readily believe that the mind in framing a Theogony, or in assigning distinct provinces to the Powers who were supposed to preside over Nature, could in its first Essays proceed with so calm and deliberate a pace through the fields of invention, as that its work should be the perfect pattern of just and corrected composition.

From these observations laid together, your Lordship will judge of the state of Lyric Poetry, when it was first introduced, and will perhaps be inclined to assent to a part of the proposition laid down in the beginning, "that as Poets in general are more apt to set up a false standard xiv of excellence than Philosophers are, so the Lyric Poet was exposed to this danger more immediately than any other member of the same profession." Whether or not the preceding Theory can be justly applied to the works of the first Lyric Poets, and how far the Ode continued to be characterised by it in the more improved state of ancient Learning, are questions which can only be answered by taking a short view of both.

It is indeed, my Lord, much to be regretted, that we have no *certain guide* to lead us through that labyrinth in which we *grope for the discovery* of Truth, and are so often *entangled in the maze* of Error when we attempt to explain the origin of Science, or to trace the manners of remote antiquity. Ishould be at a loss to enter upon this perplexed and intricate subject, if I did not know, that History has already familiarized to your Lordship the principal objects which occur in this research, and that it is the effect of extensive knowledge and superior penetration to invigorate the effort of Diffidence, and to repress the surmises of undistinguishing Censure.

The Inhabitants of Greece who make so eminent a figure in the records of Science, as well as in the History of the progression of Empire, were originally a savage and lawless people, who lived in a state of war with one another, and possessed a desolate country, from which xv they expected to be driven by the invasion of a foreign enemy14. Even after they had begun to emerge from this state of absolute barbarity, and had built a kind of cities to restrain the encroachments of the neighbouring nations, the inland country continued to be laid waste by the depredations of robbers, and the maritime towns were exposed to the incursions of pirates15. Ingenious as this people naturally were, the terror and suspence in which they lived for a considerable time, kept them unacquainted with the Arts and Sciences which were flourishing in other countries. When therefore a Genius capable of civilizing them started up, it is no wonder that they held him in the highest estimation, and concluded that he was either descended from, or inspired by some of those Divinities whose praises he was employed in rehearsing.

Such was the situation of Greece, when Linus, Orpheus, and Museus, the first Poets whose names have reached posterity, made their appearance on the theatre of life. These writers undertook the difficult task of reforming their countrymen, and of laying down a theological and philosophical system16. —We are informed by xvi Diogenes Laertius, that Linus, the Father of Grecian Poetry, was the son of Mercury and the Muse Urania, and that he sung of the Generation of the world, of the course of the sun and moon, of the origin of animals, and of the principles of vegetation17. He taught, says the same Author, that all things were formed at one time, and that they were jumbled together in a Chaos, till the operation of a Mind introduced regularity.

After all, however, we must acknowledge, that so complex, so diversified, and so ingenious a system as the Greek Theology, was too much for an *uninstructed* Genius, however exuberant, to have conceived in its full extent. Accordingly we are told, that both Orpheus and Museus travelled into Ægypt, and infused the traditionary learning of a cultivated people into the minds of their own illiterate countrymen18. To do this the more effectually, they composed Hymns, or short sonnets, in which their meaning was couched under the veil of beautiful allegory, that their lessons might at once arrest the xviid imagination, and be impressed upon the Memory19. This, my Lord, we are informed by the great Critic, was the first dress in which Poetry made its appearance20.

Of Orpheus we know little more with certainty, than that the subjects of his poems were the formation of the world, the offspring of Saturn, the birth of the Giants, and the origin of man21. These were favourite topics among the first Poets, and the discussion of them tended at once to enlarge the imagination, and to give the reasoning faculty a proper degree of exercise. This Poet however, though he obtained the highest honours from his contemporaries, yet seems to have managed his subjects in so loose a manner, that succeeding Writers will not allow him to have been a Philosopher22. At present we are not sufficiently qualified to determine his character, as most of the pieces which pass under his name are ascribed to one Onomacritus, an Athenian who flourished about the time of Pisistratus. That the writings of Orpheus were highly and extensively useful, is a truth confirmed by the most convincing evidence. The extraordinary xviii effects which his Poetry and Music are said to have produced, however absurd and incredible in themselves, are yet unquestioned proofs that he was considered as a superior Genius, and

that his countrymen thought themselves highly indebted to him.
Horace gives an excellent account of this matter in very few words.

Sylvestres homines, Sacer, Interpresque Deorum

Cædibus, & victu fœdo deterruit Orpheus,

Dictus ob hoc lenire tigres, rabidosque leones.23

The wood-born race of men when Orpheus tam'd,

From acorns, and from mutual blood reclaim'd.

The Priest divine was fabled to assuage

The tiger's fierceness, and the lion's rage. Francis.

Museus, the Pupil of Orpheus, is as little known to posterity as
his Master. His only genuine production which has reached the
present times is an Ode to Ceres, a piece indeed full of exuberance
and variety24. The Ancients in general seem to have entertained a
very high opinion of his Genius and writings, as he is said to have
been the first person who composed a regular Theogony, and is
likewise celebrated as the inventor of the Sphere25. His principle
xixd2 was that all things would finally resolve into the same materials of which they were originally compounded26. Virgil assigns him
a place of distinguishied eminence in the plains of Elysium.

− −sic est affata Sibylla.

Musæum ante omnes, medium nam plurima turba

Hunc habet, atque humeris extantem suspicit altis.27

− −The Sibyl thus address'd

Musæus, rais'd o'er all the circling throng.

It is generally allowed that Amphion, who was a native of Bæotia,
brought music into Greece from Lydia, and invented that instrument (the Lyre) from which Lyric Poetry takes its name28. Before
his time they had no xx regular knowledge of this divine art, though
we must believe that they were acquainted with it in some measure,
as dancing is an art in which we are informed that the earliest Poets
were considerable proficients29.

Such, my Lord, was the character of the first Lyric Poets, and such
were the subjects upon which they exercised invention. We have

seen, in the course of this short detail, that these Authors attempted to civilize a barbarous people, whose imagination it was necessary to seize by every possible expedient; and upon whom chastised composition would have probably lost its effect, as its beauties are not perceptible to the rude and illiterate. That they employed this method principally to instruct their countrymen is more probable, when we remember that the rudiments of learning were brought from Ægypt, a country in which Fable and Allegory remarkably xxi predominated30. By conversing with this people, it is natural to suppose that men of impetuous imaginations would imbibe their manner, and would adopt that species of composition as the most proper, which was at the same time agreeable to their own inclination, and authorised as expedient by the example of others.

From the whole, my Lord, we may conclude with probability, that the Greek Hymn was originally a loose allegorical Poem, in which Imagination was permitted to take its full career, and sentiment was rendered at once obscure and agreeable, by being screened behind a veil of the richest poetic imagery.

The loose fragments of these early writers which have come down to our times, render this truth as conspicuous as the nature of the subject will permit. A Theogony, or an account of the procession of fabulous Deities, was a theme on which Imagination might display her inventive power in its fullest extent. Accordingly Hesiod introduces his work with recounting the genealogy of the Muses, to whom he assigns "an apartment and attendants, near the summit of snowy Olympus31." These Ladies, xxii he tells us, "came to pay him a visit, and complimented him with a scepter and a branch of laurel, when he was feeding his flock on the mountain of Helicon32." Some tale of this kind it was usual with the Poets to invent, that the vulgar in those ages of fiction and ignorance might consider their persons as sacred, and that the *offspring of their imaginations* might be regarded as *the children of Truth*.

From the same licentious use of Allegory and Metaphor sprung the Fables of the wars of the Giants, of the birth and education of Jupiter, of the dethroning of Saturn, and of the provinces assigned by the Supreme to the Inferior Deities; all of which are subjects said to have been particularly treated by Orpheus33. The love of Fable became indeed so remarkably prevalent in the earliest ages, that it is now impossible in many instances to distinguish real from apparent truth in the History of these times, and to discriminate the persons who were useful members of society, from those who exist only in the works of a Poet, whose aim was professedly to excite Admiration. Thus every event of importance was disfigured by the colouring of poetic narration, and by ascribing to one man the separate actions which perhaps were xxiii performed by several persons of one name34, we are now wholly unable to disentangle truth from a perplexed and complicated detail of real and fictitious incidents.

It appears likewise from these shreds of antiquity, that the subjects of the Hymn were not sufficiently limited, as we sometimes find one of them addressed to several Deities, whose different functions recurring constantly to the mind must have occasioned unavoidable obscurity35. The Poet by this means was led into numberless digressions, in which the remote points of connection will be imperceptible to the reader, who cannot place himself in some situation similar to that of the Writer, and attend particularly to the character and manners of the period at which he wrote.

xxiv

Your Lordship, without the testimony of experience, would hardly believe that a species of composition which derived its origin from, and owed its peculiarities to the circumstances we have mentioned, could have been considered in an happier æra as a pattern worthy the imitation of cultivated genius, and the perusal of a polished and civilized people. One is indeed ready to conclude, at the first view, that a mode of writing which was assumed for a particular purpose, and was adopted to the manners of an illiterate age, might at least have undergone considerable alterations in succeeding periods, and might have received improvements proportioned to those which are made in other branches of the same art. But the fact is, that while the other branches of poetry have been gradually modelled by the rules of criticism, the Ode hath only been changed in a few external circumstances, and the enthusiasm, obscurity and exuberance, which characterised it when first introduced, continue to be ranked among its capital and discriminating excellencies.

To account for this phenomenon, my Lord, Ineed only remind your Lordship of a truth which reflexion has, no doubt, frequently suggested; — that the rules of criticism are originally drawen, not from the speculative idea of perfection in an art, but from the work of that Artist to whom either merit or accident hath appropriated xxve the most established character. From this position it obviously follows, that such an art must arrive at once to its highest perfection, as the attempts of succeeding performers are estimated not by their own intrinsic *value* or demerit, but by their conformity to a standard which is previously set before them. It hath happened fortunately for the republic of letters, that the two higher species of poetry are exempted from the bad consequences which might have followed an exact observation of this rule. An early and perfect standard was settled to regulate the Epopee, and the Drama was susceptible of *gradual improvement*, as Luxury augmented the subjects, and decorated the machinery of the theatre. We have already seen that Lyric Poetry was not introduced with the advantages of the former, and reflection must convince us, that it is not calculated to gain the slow and imperceptible accessions of the latter. We may observe however in the general, that as the opinions of the bulk of mankind in speculative matters are commonly the result of accident rather than the consequences of reflection, so it becomes extremely difficult, if not impossible, in some instances to point out a defect in an *established model* without incurring the censure of the multitude. Such, my Lord, is the nature of man, and so trifling and capricious are the circumstances upon which his sentiments depend.

xxvi

Accustomed as your Lordship has been to survey the improved manners of an enlightned age, you will contemplate with pleasure an happier aera in the progression of Science, when the Ode from being confined wholly to fictitious Theology, was transposed to the circle of Elegance and the Graces. Such is its appearance in the writings ot Anacreon, of Horace, and in the two fragments of Sappho.

Anacreon was nearly contemporary with that Onomacritus, whom we have mentioned as the Author of those poems which are ascribed to Orpheus. He flourished between the 60th and the 70th Olympiad. His pieces are the offspring of genius and indolence. His subjects are perfectly suited to his character. The devices which he would have to be carved upon a silver cup are extremely ingenious.

— —Διος γονον

Βακχον Ευιον ἡμιν.

Μυστιν αματε Κυπριν

Ὑμεναιοις κροτουσαν.

Και Εροτας αποπλους

Και χαριτας γελωσας, &c.36

— —The race of Jove,

Bacchus whose happy smiles approve;

xxviie2

The Cyprian Queen, whose gentle hand

Is quick to tye the nuptial band;

The sporting Loves unarm'd appear,

The Graces loose and laughing near.

Sweetness and natural elegance characterise the writings of this Poet, as much as carelessness and ease distinguished his manners. In some of his pieces there is exuberance and even wildness of imagination, as in that particularly which is addressed to a young girl, where he wishes alternately to be transformed into a mirror, a coat, a stream, a bracelet, and a pair of shoes, for the different purposes which he recites37. This is meer sport and wantonness, and the Poet would probably have excused himself for it, by alledging that he took no greater liberties in his own sphere than his predecessors of the same profession had done in another. His indolence and love of ease is often painted with great simplicity and elegance38, and his writings abound with those beautiful and unexpected turns which are characteristic of every species of the Ode39.

xxviii

Though we must allow Anacreon to have been an original Genius, yet it is probable, as I formerly observed, that he took Lyric Poetry as he found it; and without attempting to correct imperfections, of which he might have been sensible, made on the contrary the same use of this which a man of address will do of the foibles of his neighbour, by employing them to promote his own particular purposes. We may conclude indeed from the character of this Poet, that he was not fitted to strike out new lights in the field of Science, or to make considerable deviations from the practice of his Predecessors. He was, no doubt, of opinion likewise, that his manner was authorised in some measure by the example of the Mitylenian Poetess, whose pieces are celebrated for softness and delicacy40, and who possessed above all others the art of selecting the happiest circumstances which she placed likewise in the most striking points of view41. Longinus produceth, as a proof of this, her fine Ode inscribed to a favourite attendant, in which the progression of that tumultuous emotion, which deprived her of her senses, is described with peculiar elegance and sensibility42.

xxix

We are at a loss to judge of the character of Alcæus, the countryman and rival of Sappho, because scarce any fragment of his writings has reached the present times. He is celebrated by the Ancients as a spirited Author, whose poems abounded with examples of the sublime and vehement. Thus Horace says, when comparing him to Sappho, that he sung so forcibly of wars, disasters, and shipwrecks, that the Ghosts stood still to hear him in silent astonishment43. The same Poet informs us, that he likewise sung of Bacchus, Venus, the Muses, and Cupid44. From these sketches of his character we may conclude that his pieces were distinguished by those marks of rapid and uncontrolled imagination, which we have found to characterise the works of the first Lyric Poets.

Your Lordship needs not be told, that the Roman Poet who had the advantage of improving upon so many originals, takes in a greater variety of subjects than any of xxx his predecessors, and runs into more diffuse and diversified measure. Ihave said, my Lord, that his subjects are more diversified, because in the character of a Lyric Poet we must consider him as a professed imitator both of Anacreon and of Pindar. In the former point of view he falls under our immediate cognisance; in the latter we shall take a view of him afterwards, when we come to examine the works of that great Original, whose example he follows.

The Reader will observe, that in the shorter Odes of Horace there is commonly one leading thought, which is finely enlivened with the graces of description. Aconstant Unity of sentiment is therefore preserved in each of them, and the abrupt starts and sallies of passion are so artfully interwoven with the principal subject, that upon a review of the whole piece, we find it to be a perfect imitation of Nature. This Poet (whose judgment appears to have been equal to his imagination) is particularly careful to observe propriety in his most irregular excursions, and the vivacity of his passion is justified by the circumstances in which he is supposed to be placed. The diction of these poems is likewise adapted with great accuracy to the sentiment, as it is generally concise, forcible, and expressive. Brevity of language ought indeed particularly to characterise this species of the Ode, in which the Poet writes from immediate feeling, and is intensely xxxi animated by his subject. Delicacy is likewise indispensibly requisite, because the reader is apt to be disgusted with the least appearance of constraint or harshness in a poem, whose principal excellence lies in the happy and elegant turn of a pointed reflection. In short, little sallies and picturesque epithets have a fine effect in pieces of this kind, as by the former the passions are forcibly inflamed, and by the latter their effects are feelingly exposed.

Of all these delicate beauties of composition, the Odes of Horace abound with pregnant and striking examples. Sometimes he discovers the strength of his passion, when he is endeavouring to forget it, by a sudden and lively turn which is wholly unexpected. Thus he tells Lydia,

Non si me satis audias,

Speres perpetuum dulcia barbare

Lædentem oscula, quæ Venus

Quinta parte sui nectaris imbuit.45

Sometimes his pictures are heightned with beautiful imagery, and he seizeth the imagination before he appeals to reason. Thus, when he is advising his friend not to mourn any longer for a man who was dead, instead of proposing the subject immediately he says,

xxxii

Non semper imbres nubibus hispidos

Manant in agros, &c.46

Not always snow, and hail, and rain

Defend, and beat the fruitful plain. CREECH.

On other occasions he breaks abruptly into a short and spirited transition.

Auditis? an me ludit amabilis

Insania? audire et videor pios

Errare per lucos, amœnæ

Quos et aquae subeunt et auræ.47

Dos't hear? or sporting in my brain,

What wildly-sweet deliriums reign!

Lo! mid Elysium's balmy groves,

Each happy shade transported roves!

I see the living scene display'd,

Where rills and breathing gales sigh murmuring thro' the shade.

On some subjects he is led imperceptibly into a soft melancholy, which peculiar elegance of expression renders extremely agreeable in the end of this poem. There is a fine stroke of this kind in his Ode to Septimus, with whom he was going to fight against the Cantabrians. He figures out a poetical recess for his old age, and then says,

xxxiiif

Ille te mecum locus, et beatæ

Postulant arces, ibi tu calentem

Debita sparges lachryma favillam

Vatis amici.48

That happy place, that sweet retreat.

The charming hills that round it rise,

Your latest hours, and mine await;

And when your Poet Horace dyes;

There the deep sigh thy poet-friend shall mourn,

And pious tears bedew his glowing urn. Francis.

Upon the whole, my Lord, you will perhaps be of opinion, that though the subjects of this second species of the Ode are wholly different from these of the first; yet the same variety of images, boldness of transition, figured diction, and rich colouring which characterised this branch of poetry on its original introduction, continue to be uniformly and invariably remarkable in the works of succeeding performers. Reflection indeed will induce us to acknowledge, that in this branch of Lyric Poetry the Author may be allowed to take greater liberties than we could permit him to do in that which has formerly been mentioned. It is the natural effect of any passion by which the mind is agitated, to break out into short and abrupt sallies which are expressive of its impetuosity, and of an imagination heated, and starting in the xxxiv tumult of thought from one object to another. To follow therefore the workings of the mind in such a situation and to paint them happily, is in other words to copy Nature. But your Lordship will observe, that the transitions of the Poet who breaks from his subject to exhibit an historical detail whose connection with it is remote, or who is solicitous to display the fertility of a rich imagination at the expence of perspicuity, when it is not supposed that his passions are inflamed: you will observe, my Lord, that his digressions are by no means so excusable as those of the other, because obscurity in the latter may be an excellence, whereas in the former it is always a blemish.

It is only necessary to observe farther on this head, that the difference of the subjects treated by Anacreon and Horace, from those of Orpheus, Museus, &c. is owing to the different characters of the ages in which they lived. We could not indeed have expected to meet with any thing very serious, at any period, from so indolent and careless a writer as Anacreon. But Luxury even in his time had made considerable progress in the world. The principles of Theology were sufficiently well established. Civil polity had succeeded to a state of confusion, and men were become fond of ease and affluence, of wine and women. Anacreon lived at the court of a voluptuous Monarch49, and had nothing to divert his mind from xxxvf2 the pursuit of happiness in his own way. His Odes therefore are of that kind, in which the gentler Graces peculiarly predominate. Sappho and Horace were employed in the same manner. The Lady had a Gallant, of whom it appears that she was extremely fond, and the Roman Poet lived in a polite court, was patronized by a man of distinguished eminence, and was left at full liberty to pursue that course of life to which he was most powerfully prompted by inclination.

The poetic vein in these Writers takes that turn, which a stranger must have expected upon hearing their characters. Their pieces are gay, entertaining, loose, elegant, and ornamented with a rich profusion of the graces of description. The reader of sensibility will receive the highest pleasure from perusing their works, in which the internal movements of the mind warmed by imagination, or agitated by passion, are exposed in the happiest and most agreeable attitudes. This, perhaps, is the principal excellence of the looser branches of poetic composition. The mind of the Poet in these pieces is supposed to be intensely kindled by his subject. His Fancy assumes the rein, and the operation of reason is for a moment suspended. He follows the impulse of enthusiasm, and throws off those simple but lively strokes of Nature and Passion, which can only be felt, and are beyond imitation.

xxxvi
Ut sibi quivis

Speret idem, sudet multum, frustraque laboret

Ausus idem!50

All may hope to imitate with ease:

Yet while they drive the same success to gain,

Shall find their labour and their hopes are vain. Francis.

The unequal measures which are used in these shorter Odes, are likewise adapted with great propriety to the subjects of which they treat. Horace says, that this inequality of numbers was originally fixed upon as expressive of the complaints of a lover; but he adds, that they became quickly expressive likewise of his exultation.

Versibus impariter junctis Querimonia primum

Post etiam inclusa est voti sententia compos.51

Unequal measures first were taught to flow,

Sadly expressive of the Lover's woe.

These looser and shorter measures distinguish this branch of the Ode from the Hymn which was composed in heroic measure52, and from the Pindaric Ode (as it is commonly called) to which the dithyrambique or more diversified stanza was particularly appropriated. Of the shorter Ode therefore it may be said with propriety,

xxxvii

Son stile impetueux souvent marche au hazarde

Chez un beau disordre est un effect de l'art.53

Thus, my Lord, we have taken a view of the Lyric poetry of the Ancients, as it appeared originally in the works of the earliest Poets, and as it was afterwards employed to enliven a train of more elegant and delicate sentiment. Ihave attempted, in the course of this enquiry, to follow the lights which Antiquity throws on this subject as closely as possible, to explain facts by placing them in connection, and to illustrate reasoning by example.

Your Lordship's acquaintance with the principles of civil Government, and your experience of the effects of education have enabled you to observe the *character*, which the Manners *of an age* stamp upon the productions of the Authors who live in it. Experience will convince us, that these general revolutions resemble more nearly than we are apt to imagine at first view, the circumstances of an Individual at the different periods of life. In one age he is captivated by the beauties of description, at another he is fond of the deductions of Philosophy; his opinions vary with his years, and his actions, as directed by these, are proportionably diversified. In all these circumstances however, the original bias which he received from Nature remains unalterable, and the peculiarity of his character appears conspicuous, notwithstanding xxxviii the accidental diversity of fluctuating sentiments. It is to be expected in such a situation, that changes similar to these will usually take place in arts which are susceptible of perpetual mutation; and of this a particular instance is exhibited in the preceding detail. Another branch of this subject remains to be considered, and on this I shall give your Lordship the trouble of perusing a few remarks in a subsequent letter. Permit me only to observe, from what hath already been advanced, that the ingredients of Genius are often bestowed by Nature, when the polish of Art is wanted to mould the original materials into elegant proportion. He who possesseth the former in the highest degree may be a Shakespear or an Æschylus; but both were united in forming the more perfect characters of Demosthenes and Homer.

xxxix

LETTER II.

The view, my Lord, of the Lyric Poetry of the Ancients which has been taken in the preceding part of this Essay, may probably have suggested a Question to your Lordship, to which it is necessary that an answer should be given, before I enter upon that part of the subject which remains to be considered. From the observations formerly made, Iam afraid that your Lordship has been looking upon my procedure, as you would have viewed that of the honest Irishman, who pulled an old house about his ears, before he had reflected that it was necessary to substitute a better in its room. In the same manner you will perhaps think, that I have taken a good deal of pains to point out the *Defects* of Lyric Poetry, and to assign the *Causes* which originally produced them; without however establishing the rules of this branch of the Art, and without enquiring what proportion of poetic embellishment naturally belongs to it, considered as distinguished from every other species.

xl

Permit me therefore to observe, that my intention in the preceding remarks will be greatly mistaken, if, when I have been endeavouring to expose the *abuse* of imagination, it should be thought, either that I would wholly repress the excursions of this noble Faculty, or that I would confine its exercise within narrow limits. It must be obvious to every person who reflects on this subject, that Imagination presides over every branch of the Poetic Art, and that a certain infusion of her peculiar beauties is necessary to constitute its real and essential character. The Poet therefore of every denomination may be said with great propriety in an higher sense than the Orator, "to paint to the eyes, and touch the soul, and combat with shining arms54." It is from this consideration that Horace says, speaking of Poetry in general,

Descriptas servare vices, operumque colores,

Cur ego si nequeo ignoroque, Poeta salutor?55

Though the influence of imagination on every species of Poetry is so obvious, as not to stand in need of illustration, yet we must observe at the same time, that xlig this power is exerted in different degrees56, as the Poet is led by the nature of that subject to which his Genius hath received the most remarkable bias. Thus the simple beauties of the Eclogue would appear in the same light, when transposed to the Epopee, as plants brought to forced vegetation in a Green-house must do to those who have seen them flourishing in their native soil, and ripened by the benignity of an happier climate. In the one case they are considered as unnatural productions, whose beauty is surpassed by the Natives of the soil; in the other they are regarded as just and decent ornaments, whose real excellence is properly estimated. The same remark may be applied indiscriminately to all the other branches of this art. Though they are originally the offspring of *one Parent*, yet there are certain characteristic marks, by which a general resemblance is fully distinguished from perfect similarity.

It is necessary to observe in general on this subject, that whatever degree of superiority the reasoning Faculty ought ultimately to possess in the sphere of Composition, we are not to consider this Power as acting the same part in the work of a Poet, which it should always act in that of a Philosopher. In the performance of the latter, an appeal to reason is formally stated, and is carried on by the xlii process of connected argumentation; whereas in that of the former the Judgment is *principally* employed in the disposition of materials57. Thus the Philosopher and the Poet are equally entitled to the character of judicious, when the arguments of the one are just and conclusive, and when the images of the other are apposite and natural.

xliiig2

When your Lordship reflects on the Nature and End of Lyric Poetry, it will appear to be at least as much characterised by the Graces of ornament as any other species whatever. We have already seen that the Ode was early consecrated to the purposes of Religion, and that it was intended to raise Admiration by extolling the attributes of the Supreme Being. On a subject of this nature the Poet probably thought, that sublime and exuberant imagery was necessary to support the grandeur of those sentiments which were naturally suggested to his mind58. Even when these original topics were laid aside, and the Lyric Muse acted in another sphere, her strains were still employed, either to commemorate the actions of Deified Heroes, or to record the exploits of persons whom rank and abilities rendered eminently conspicuous.

All these subjects afford a noble field for the play of imagination, and it is a certain truth that the purity of composition is generally defective, in proportion to that degree of sublimity at which the Poet is capable of arriving59. Great objects are apt to confound and dazzle xliv the imagination. In proportion as this faculty expands to take them in, its power of conceiving them distinctly becomes less adequate to the subject; and when the mind is overwrought and drained as it were of sentiment, it is no wonder that we find it sometimes attempting to repair this loss, by substituting in the room of true sublimity an affected pomp and exuberance of expression.

That we may conceive more fully the propriety of this observation with regard to Lyric Poetry, Ishall now proceed to enquire what part Imagination naturally claims in the composition of the Ode, and what are the errors into which the Poet is most ready to be betrayed.

As to the first, I need not tell your Lordship, that whatever Art proposeth as an ultimate end to excite Admiration, must owe its principal excellence to that Faculty of the mind which delights to contemplate the sublime and the wonderful. This indeed may be called the sphere, in which Imagination peculiarly predominates. When we attempt, even in the course of conversation, to paint any object whose magnificence hath made a strong impression upon the memory, we naturally adopt the boldest and most forcible epithets we can think of, to convey our own idea as compleatly as possible to the mind of another. We are prompted by a powerful propensity to retouch our description again and again, we select the most apposite images to animate our expression; in short, xlv we fall without perceiving it, into the stile and figures of poetry. If then Admiration produceth such an effect upon the mind in the more common occurrences of life, we may conceive the superior influence which it must have upon the imagination of a Poet, when it is wound up to the highest pitch, and is placing a great object in every point of light by which its excellence may most conspicuously appear. It will at least be obvious, that in such a situation the feelings of the heart must be more intensely animated than in any other, not only because Genius is supposed to be the Parent of Sensibility, but as the person who is possessed of this quality exerts the full force of his talents and art to produce one particular effect. He endeavours (as Longinus expresseth it) "not to be seen himself, but to place the idea which he hath formed before the very eye of another60."

It is a common mistake among people who have not examined this subject, to suppose that a Poet may with greater ease excite Admiration when his theme is sublime, than when it is such as we have been more accustomed to contemplate61. This opinion is indeed plausible at the first view, because it may be said that xlvi we go half-way to meet that Author, who proposeth to reach an end by means which have an apparent probability to effectuate it; but it will appear upon reflection, that this very circumstance, instead of being serviceable, is in reality detrimental to the Poet.

Admiration is a passion which can never be excited in any person, unless when there is something great and astonishing, either in the general disposition of a work or in some of the separate members of which it is formed. Thus we admire a whole piece, when we observe that the parts which compose it are placed in a striking and uncommon combination, and we even consider one happy stroke as an indication of genius in the Artist. It frequently happens that the subject of a Poem is of such a nature, as that its most essential members cannot be set in any light distinct from that in which custom and experience has led us to consider them. Thus when the Poet addressed an Hymn to Jupiter, Diana, or Apollo, he could not be ignorant that his readers were well apprised of the general manner, in which it was necessary to treat of these Personages, and that they would have been offended, if he had presumed to differ in any material point from the opinions handed down by traditionary evidence. It was therefore necessary, that the Poet should manage a subject of this kind in the same manner as Rubens and Caypel have painted the Crucifixion, by either varying *the attitude* of the principal object to make it more sublime and admirable, or by rendering some *inferior figure* picturesque and animated which had escaped the notice of his Predecessors. When therefore a sublime object is not shown in some great and uncommon point of view, the Poet sinks in our esteem as much as he would have risen in it, if we had found his Genius equal to his Ambition.

As I have already borrowed one illustration from painting, permit me to recall to your Lordship's memory, that noble figure by which the Church of Rome permitted Raphael to represent the Eternal Father, a figure which has always been considered as one of the greatest ornaments of the galleries of the Vatican62. Any person may conclude that the difficulty of succeeding in this great attempt, must have bore some proportion to the *temerity* (shall we call it) of venturing to design it. If this celebrated Artist had failed of throwing into that figure an Air wholly extraordinary, his Design would either have been considered as rash, or his imagination censured as deficient.

On the contrary, the Poet who chuseth a more unpromising subject, and displays an unexpected fertility of invention xlviii in his manner of treating it, is admired as an Original Genius, and the perusal of his work excites in our mind the most agreeable mixture of surprize and pleasure.

It must immediately occur to any reader who peruseth the Hymn of Callimachus to Jupiter, that the subject was too great to be properly managed by the correct and elegant genius of that writer. Instead of enlarging (as we should have naturally expected) on any particular perfection of this Supreme Deity, or even of enumerating in a poetical manner the attributes which were commonly ascribed to Him, he entertains us coldly with traditionary stories about His birth and education; and the sublime part of his subject is either wholly omitted, or superficially passed over. Thus speaking of the bird of Jove, he says only,

Θηκαο δ' οιωνον μεγ' ὑπειροχον αγγελεωτην,

Σων τερααων· ἁτ' εμοισι φιλοις ενδεξια φαινοις.63

Thy bird, celestial messenger, who bears

Thy mandate thro' the sky;—O be his flight

Propitious to my friends!

Pindar introduceth this King of the feathered race in a much nobler and more animated manner. He exhibits with true poetic enthusiasm, as an instance of the power of harmony, the following vivid picture.

xlixh

— — — — — εὐ-

δει ανα σκαπτω Διος αιετος, ω-

κειαν πτερυγ' αμφοτερω-

θεν χαλαξεις,

Αρχος αιωνων· — —

— — ὁ δε κνωσσων

ὑγρον νωτον αιωρει, τεαις

ρεπαισι κατασχομενος.64

The birds fierce Monarch drops his vengeful ire;

Perch'd on the sceptre of the Olympian King,

The thrilling darts of harmony he feels,

And indolently hangs his rapid wing,

While gentle sleep his closing eye-lids seals;

And o'er his heaving limbs, in loose array

To every balmy gale the ruffling feathers play. West.

Homer never touches this sublime subject, without employing the utmost reach of his invention to excite admiration in his reader.

Ζευς δε Πατηρ ιδηθεν ευτροχον ἁρμα και ἱππους

Ολυμπονδ' εδιωκε, θεων δ' εξεκετο θωκους.

Τω δε και ἱππους μεν λυσε κλυτος Εννοσιγαιος

Ἁρματα δ' αμβρωμοισι τιθει, κατα λιτα πετασσας.

Αυτος δε χρυσειον επι θρωνον ευρυοπα Ζευς

Ἑζετο, τω δε ὑπο ποσσι μεγας πελεμιζετ' Ολυμπος.65

――The Thund'rer meditates his flight

From Ida's summits to th' Olympian height.

Swifter than thought the wheels instinctive fly,

Flame thro' the vast of air, and reach the sky.

l

'Twas Neptune's charge his coursers to unbrace,

And fix the car on its immortal base, &c.

He whose all-conscious eyes the world behold,

Th' eternal Thunderer, sate thron'd in gold.

High heav'n the footstool of his feet He makes,

And wide beneath him all Olympus shakes. Pope.

I have mentioned these examples, as they shew the light in which a great object will be contemplated by a man of genius; and as the reader will observe that our admiration is not merely excited by the dignity of the theme, but that it results from the great and uncommon circumstances which are happily thrown into the description. Pindar, no doubt, found it a much easier task to raise this passion in favour of Theron, whom he artfully introduceth to the reader's attention, after enquiring of his Muse what God or what distinguished Heroe he should attempt to celebrate.66

lih2

It is however obvious, from what hath been advanced on this subject, that whatever may be the nature of the theme on which the

Poet insists, it is the business of Fancy to enliven the whole piece with those natural and animating graces which lead us to survey it with admiration. From the whole therefore it appears, that this Faculty of the mind claims an higher share of merit in the competition of the Ode than in any other species of Poetry; because in the other branches of this art different ends may be obtained, and different expedients may be fallen upon to gain them; but the most perfect kind of Lyric Poetry admits only of that end, to the attainment of which fertility of Imagination is indispensably requisite.

You will recollect, my Lord, a petition laid down in the beginning of this Essay;—that "when Imagination is permitted to bestow the graces of ornament indiscriminately, sentiments are either superficial, and thinly scattered through a work, or we are obliged to search for them beneath a load of superfluous colouring." Ishall now endeavour to evince the truth of this reflection, by enquiring more particularly what are the faults into which the Lyric Poet is most ready to be betrayed, by giving a loose rein to that Faculty which colours and enlivens his composition.

It may be observed then in general, that we usually judge of the Genius of a Lyric Poet by the variety of his lii*images*, the boldness of his *transitions*, and the picturesque vivacity of his *descriptions*. Ishall under this head trouble your Lordship with a few reflections on each of these considered separately.

By the Images which are employed in the Ode, Imean those illustrations borrowed from *natural* and often from *familiar* objects, by which the Poet either clears up an obscurity, or arrests the attention, and kindles the imagination of his reader. These illustrations have very distinct uses in the different species of poetic composition. The greatest Masters in the Epopee often introduce metaphors, which have only a general relation to the subject; and by pursuing these through a variety of circumstances, they disengage the reader's attention from the principal object. This indeed often becomes necessary in pieces of length, when attention begins to relax by following too closely one particular train of ideas. It requires however great judgment in the Poet to pursue this course with approbation, as he must not only fix upon metaphors which in some points have a striking similarity to the object illustrated, but even the digressive circumstances must be so connected with it, as to exhibit a succession of sentiments which resemble, at least remotely, the subject of his Poem67. It must be obvious, at first liii view, that as the Lyric Poet cannot adopt this plea, his metaphors will always have the happiest effect, when they correspond to the object in such a manner, as to shew its compleat proportions in the fullest point of view, without including foreign and unappropriated epithets. This however is not the course which a Writer of imagination will naturally follow, unless his judgment restrains the excursions of that excentric faculty. He will, on the contrary, catch with eagerness every image which Fancy enlivens with the richest colouring, and he will contemplate the external beauty of his metaphor, rather than consider the propriety with which it is applied as an illustration. It is probably owing to this want of just attention to propriety, that the first Lyric Poets have left such imperfect standards to the imitation of posterity.

When we examine the works of later Poets among the Ancients, we find that even those of them who are most exceptionable in other circumstances, have yet in a great measure corrected this mistake of their predecessors. In the lyric Odes of Euripides and Sophocles, the metaphors made use of are generally short, expressive, and fitted to liv correspond with great accuracy to the point which requires to be illustrated68. Pindar is in many instances equally happy in the choice of his images, which are frequently introduced with address, and produce a very striking effect69.

It is likewise necessary that the Poet should take care in the higher species of the Ode, to assign to every object that precise degree of colour, as well as that importance in the arrangement of sentiments which it seems peculiarly to demand. The same images which would be considered as capital strokes in some pieces can be admitted only as secondary beauties in others; and we might call in question both the judgment and the imagination of that Poet who attempts to render a faint illustration adequate to the object, by clothing it with profusion of lv ornament. Adefect likewise either in the choice, or in the disposition, of images, is conspicuous in proportion to the importance of the subject, as well as to the nature of those sentiments with which it stands in more immediate connection. It is therefore the business of the Lyric Poet, who would avoid the censure of competing with inequality, to consider the colouring of which particular ideas are naturally susceptible, and to discriminate properly betwixt sentiments, whose native sublimity requires but little assistance from the pencil of art, and a train of thought which (that it may correspond to the former) demands the heightening of poetic painting. The astonishing inequalities which we meet with, even in the productions of unquestioned Genius, are originally to be deduced from the carelessness of the Poet who permitted his imagination to be hurried from one object to another, dwelling with pleasure upon a favourite idea, and passing slightly over intermediate steps, that he may catch that beauty which fluctuates on the gaze of Expectation.

I shall only observe further on this subject, that nothing is more contrary to the end of Lyric Poetry, than that habit of spinning out a metaphor which a Poet sometimes falls into by indulging the sallies of imagination. This will be obvious, when we reflect that every branch of the Ode is characterised by a peculiar degree of vivacity and even vehemence both of sentiment and expression. lvi It is impossible to preserve this distinguishing character, unless the thoughts are diversified, and the diction is concise. When a metaphor is hunted down (if I may use that expression) and a description overwrought, its force and energy are gradually lessened, the object which was originally new becomes familiar, and the mind is satiated instead of being inflamed.

We must not think that this method of extending an illustration discovers always a defect or sterility of the inventive Faculty. It is, in truth, the consequence of that propensity which we naturally feel to consider a favourite idea in every point of light, and to render its excellence as conspicuous to others as it is to ourselves. By this means sentiments become *superficial*, because the mind is more intent upon their *external dress*, that their *real importance*. They are likewise *thinly scattered through a work*, because each of them receives an higher proportion or ornament than justly belongs to it. We frequently judge of them likewise, in the same manner as a birthday suit is estimated by its purchaser, not by the standard of intrinsic value, but by the opinion of the original proprietor. Thus to superficial readers,

— — —verbum emicuit si forte decorum,

Si versus paulo concinnior unus aut alter

Injuste totum ducit, venditque poema.70

lviii

One simile that solitary shines

In the dry desart of a thousand lines,

Or lengthen'd thought that gleams thro' many a page,

Has sanctified whole poems for an age. Pope.

Custom, my Lord, that sovereign arbiter, from whose decision in literary as well as in civil causes, there frequently lies no appeal, will lead us to consider boldness of transition as a circumstance which is peculiarly characteristic of the Ode. Lyric Poets have in all ages appropriated to themselves the liberty of indulging imagination in her most irregular excursions; and when a digression is remotely similar to the subject, they are permitted to fall into it at any time by the invariable practice of their Predecessors. Pindar expressly lays claim to this privilege.

Εγκαμιων γαρ αωτες ὑμνων

επ' αλλοτ' αλλον ως τε με-

λισσα θυνει λογον.71

The song that spreads some glorious name

Shifts its bold wing from theme to theme;

Roves like the bee regardless o'er,

And culls the spoils of every flower.

We must indeed acknowledge in general, that when an high degree of spirit and vivacity is required to characterize any species of composition, the Author may be lviii allowed to take greater liberties than we should grant to another, whose subject demanded regularity and connection. Let it however be observed at the same time, that this freedom is often granted, not because the theme indispensibly requires, but because we naturally expect it from the genius of the Writer. We justly suppose, that the Philosopher seldom mistakes his talents so far as to be solicitous of shining in a sphere, for which he must know himself to be wholly disqualified; and from the work of a Poet who addresseth imagination, we look for those marks of wildness and incoherence which discover the extent of that faculty.

I have acknowledged in a former part of this Essay, that the shorter Ode not only admits of bold and spirited transitions, but that these are in many instances necessary to constitute a perfect imitation of nature72. This observation however cannot be applied with so much propriety to the other kinds of it, because the transport of passion is abrupt, instantaneous, and the mind returns suddenly to the point from which it had digressed. On the contrary, as the passions cannot be kept on their full stretch for any considerable time, we expect that in the higher species of Lyric Poetry, the Poet will keep the principal object more immediately in his eye, and that his transitions will never make us lose sight of it so far, as lixi2 not to recall with ease the intermediate points of connection.

When this rule is not violated, we can enter with pleasure into the design of the Poet, and consider his work as a whole in which every separate member has its distinct and proper use. Thus, when Pindar is celebrating Aristagoras, we can easily observe that the Poet's oblique encomium on the Father and friends of his Heroe, is introduced with great propriety, as every remark of this kind reflects additional lustre on the character of the principal personage73. We are even sometimes highly entertained with digressions, which have not so near a relation to the subject of the Ode as the last mentioned circumstance; because though the immediate design is not going forward, we can still however keep it in view with the same ease, as a traveller can do the public road, from which he willingly makes an excursion to survey the neighbouring country. Thus the noble panegyric upon the whole people of Rhodes, and the account of their Founder Tlepolemus, which we meet with in the Ode inscribed to Diagoras the Rhodian; these are happy and beautiful embellishments, whose introduction enlivens the whole piece with a proper variety of objects74.

The same principle which induceth us to approve of Poet's transitions in the preceding instances, must (as lx your Lordship will immediately conceive) lead us to condemn those which are far-fetched, pursued too closely, or foreign to the subject of the poem. This is frequently the consequence of following the track of imagination with implicit compliance, as the Poet without being sensible of his mistake runs into one digression after another, until his work is made up of incoherent ideas; in which, as Horace expressethit,

velut ægri somnia vanæ

Finguntur species, ut nec pes, nec caput uni

Reddatur formæ.75

This is the character of the Ode to Thrasidæus the Theban, in which the Poet is insensibly led from one digression to another, until his readers lose sight of the principal subject which is dropped almost as soon as proposed76.

The last circumstance mentioned as characteristic of the Ode, was a certain picturesque vivacity of description. In this we permit the Lyric Poet to indulge himself with greater freedom than any other, because beauties of this kind are necessary to the end of exciting admiration. It is the peculiar province of imagination to give that life and expression to the ideas of the mind, by which Nature is most happily and judiciously imitated. By the help of this poetical magic the coldest sentiments become lxi interesting, and the most common occurrences arrest our attention. Aman of Genius, instead of laying down a series of dry precepts for the conduct of life, exhibits his sentiments in the most animating manner, by moulding them into symmetry, and superadding the external beauties of drapery and colour77. His reader by this expedient is led through an Elysium, in which his Fancy is alternately soothed and transported with a delightful succession of the most agreeable objects, whose combination at last suggests an important moral to be impressed upon the memory. The Ancients appear to have been fully sensible of the advantages of this method of illustrating truth, as the works not only of their Poets, but even those of their Philosophers and Historians abound with just and beautiful personifications78. Their two allegorical lxii Philosophers, Prodicus and Cebes, carry the matter still further, and inculcate their lessons, by substituting in place of cool admonition a variety of personages, who assume the most dignified character, and address at the same time the imagination, the passions, and even the senses of mankind79. These Authors consider man as a creature possessed of different, and of limited faculties, whose actions are directed more frequently by the impulse of passion, than regulated by the dictates of reason and of truth80.

It is obvious, that in Lyric Poetry the Author cannot run into this series of methodised allegory, because the subjects of the Ode are real incidents which would be disfigured by the continued action of fictitious personages. His descriptions therefore ought to be concise, diversified, and adapted properly to that train of sentiment which he is employed to illustrate. When this is the case, we are highly entertained with frequent personifications, as these are criterions by which we estimate the genius of the Poet.

lxiii

I need not, my Lord, to suggest on this branch of my subject, that it requires the utmost delicacy to personify inanimate objects so justly, as to render them adapted in every circumstance to the occasion on which they are introduced. Your Lordship however will permit me to observe, that as the happiest effect is produced upon the mind of the reader by the judicious introduction of an ideal personage; so he is apt to be disgusted in an equal degree, when the conduct of the Poet in this instance is in the smallest measure irregular or defective. When an intellectual idea falls under the cognizance of an external sense, it is immediately surveyed with an accuracy proportioned to its importance, and to the distance at which we suppose it to be placed. We judge of Virtue and Vice, when represented as persons, in the same manner as we judge of men whose appearance is suggested by memory; and we therefore expect that these ideal figures shall be discriminated from each other by their dress, attitudes, features, and behaviour, as much as two real persons of opposite characters always are in the familiar intercourse of ordinary life. In reality we assign a particular shape, complection, and manner to the creatures of imagination, by the same rule which leads us to ascribe a certain assemblage of features to a person whom we have never seen, upon seeing his character particularly displayed, or upon listening to a minute detail of his actions. lxiv Nay, odd as it may appear, it is yet certain, that in many instances our idea of the imaginary person may be more distinct and particular than that of the real one. Thus we often find that the representation exhibited by Fancy of the figure of an Heroe, whose actions had raised admiration; Isay, we find that this representation has been wide of the truth, when we come either to see the original, or a faithful copy of it: but our ideas of imaginary persons are generally so exact, that upon seeing a group of these displayed on a plate, we are capable to give each its proper designation, as soon as we observe it. Thus Anger, Revenge, Despair, Hope, &c. can be distinguished from each other almost as easily when they are copied by the pencil, as when *we feel their influence on our own minds, or make others observe it on our actions.*

From this detail it obviously follows, that as our ideas of imaginary personages are more just and accurate, than those which are excited merely by a particular relation of the actions of real ones; so we will judge with more certainty of the precise colouring which belongs to the former, and of the propriety with which they are introduced, than we can possibly do with regard to the latter. A Painter may deceive us, by throwing into the face of an Heroe, whom we have never seen, particular marks of resolution and fortitude, which form only a part of his character. But we cannot be deceived with regard to lxvk the signatures which show the predominancy of these virtues, with whatever degree of justice they may be applied. This observation has equal force, when we refer it to the allegorical personages of the Poet. The least impropriety in the colouring, dress, or arrangement of objects, is immediately perceptible, and we pass a favourable judgment, when faults of this kind are ascribed to inattention. In short, the imaginary persons who are introduced in a poem, must on all occasions be distinguished by peculiar characters, and the manners attributed to each of them ought to be such as can be applied with no propriety to any other object. Every picture must therefore be, as Pope somewhere hasit,

Something whose truth convinc'd at sight we find.

That gives us back the image of the mind.

A little reflection will enable us to discover the reason of this difference betwixt our ideas of allegorical and of real personages. We are (as I formerly observed) often mistaken in our notions of the latter of these, because the mind cannot receive a sufficient degree of information, concerning the person, to be able to form any perfect judgment of his address or demeanour. Upon hearing, for instance, a recital of the actions of a man who is unknown to us, our idea of him is taken from the passion which appears to have predominated in his conduct; but we are not acquainted with numberless little peculiarities lxvi which enter into a complicated character, and have their corresponding expressions imprinted on the countenance. Thus when we consider only the martial exploits of the celebrated Duke de Vendome, we have the idea of an Heroe full of spirit and impetuosity; but this idea would be very imperfect as a representation of his character, if we did not know likewise that he was slovenly, voluptuous, effeminate, and profuse81.

These different ingredients, which enter into the mind of a real agent, ought likewise to be nicely estimated as to the degrees in which they predominate, before we could be properly qualified to judge of their influence on his external appearance. As it is evidently impossible that we can ever be thoroughly apprised of the former, it is therefore obvious that our judgment of the latter must be always imperfect. On the contrary, we are never at a loss to conceive a just idea of one simple expression, because the Original from which the Copy is drawn exists in our own mind. We are likewise naturally taught to distinguish properly the insignia of imaginary creatures. Thus Fear is always known by her *bristled hair*, Admiration by his *erected eyes*, Time has his *scythe* and his *hour-glass*, and Fortune (unchangeable in one sense) stands *blind* on the *globe*, to which she was exalted by Cebes82.

lxviik2

I ought, my Lord, to apologize for the length of this Digression on the nature of allegorical Persons; a subject which I have treated more particularly, as I do not remember to have seen it canvassed minutely by any Writer either ancient or modern.

I shall only observe further on this head, that though a Poet is seldom in hazard of being grossly faulty, with respect to the dress and insignia of his personages, yet intemperate imagination will induce him to use this noble figure too frequently by personifying objects of small comparative importance; or by leaving the simple and natural path, to entangle himself in the labyrinth of Fiction.

This is the fault which we have already found to characterise the writings of the first Lyric Poets, from which we should find it an hard task to vindicate their successors, even in the most improved state of ancient learning. Instead of producing examples of this intemperance, which the Greek Theology was peculiarly calculated to indulge, Ishall only observe in general, that we are mistaken in thinking that the Genius of a Poet is indicated by the diversified incidents which enter into his Fable. True Genius, even in its most early productions, be discovered rather by *vivid* and *picturesque descriptions*, than by any circumstances however extraordinary in the *narration* of *events*. It is no difficult matter to conceive a series of fictitious incidents, and to connect lxviii them together in one story, though it requires judgment to do this in such a manner, as that the whole may have some happy and continued allusion to truth. We can imagine, for instance, with great ease something as impossible as Ariosto's Magician pursuing the man who had taken off his head. But it will be found a much more difficult task, either to throw out one of those strokes of Nature which penetrate the heart, and cleave it with terror and with pity; or to paint Thought in such striking colours, as to render it immediately visible to the eye83.

lxix

The noblest instances of this personification are to be found in the Sacred Writings. Nothing can exceed the majesty, with which the descent of the Almighty is described by the Prophet Habakkuk. "Before Him (he tells us) went the Pestilence, &c." then suddenly addressing the Deity in the second person, he says "the Mountains *saw Thee*, and they *trembled*, the Overflowing of the waters *passed by*, the *Deep uttered his voice*, and *lift up his hands* on high84." In another place, the Deluge is nobly animated, in order to display the Omnipotence of God. "The waters (says the Psalmist) stood above the mountains. At thy rebuke they *fled*, at the voice of thy thunder they *hasted away*."

From this simple and impartial view of the Lyric Poetry of the Ancients, considered as one branch of a cultivated Art, your Lordship will perhaps be inclined to conclude, that in the Arts, as in the characters of men, those which are susceptible of the highest excellence, are lxx likewise frequently marked with the most striking defects. This mixture of beauty and deformity, of grandeur and meanness, which enters so often into the action as well as the speculation of mankind, ought to be considered as the characteristic of the human mind, which in the chimerical pursuit of perfection is hurried by its own impetuosity from one extreme to another. Your Lordship has, no doubt, frequently observed, that there is upon the whole a greater uniformity in the characters of men than superficial enquiry would lead us to conceive. A temptation operating forcibly on the ruling passion will produce in a temper naturally gentle and equal, an irregularity as remarkable, and sometimes carried to a greater length, than the most powerful stimulus is able to excite in a man of warm passions, and florid imagination. This is a fact, of which experience will suggest examples to every person who is conversant with mankind.

We ought not therefore to wonder, when we observe in the writings of a Great Genius beauties and blemishes blended promiscuously, and when we find the Poet's imagination distinguished only by those marks of inaccuracy which appear in the actions of others, and which are ultimately to be derived from the complicated ingredients of the human mind.

lxxi

I have been led into this train of reflection, as it will enable us to account for the inequalities which are to be met with in the writings of Pindar, exposed as they have been to the admiration, and to the censure of posterity. Whatever propriety the preceding rules may have with regard to Lyric Poetry, it is certain that this Poet is not the standard from whose work they are deduced. We have already seen that He himself disclaims all conformity to the shackles of method, and that he insists upon the privilege of giving a loose rein to the excursions of imagination. The consequences of this proceeding are eminently conspicuous in every part of his writings. His composition is coloured with that rich imagery which Fancy throws upon the coldest sentiments, his digressions are often too frequent and but remotely connected with the principal subject, his personifications are bold and exuberant, and he has made as free an use of theological fable as any Poet among the Ancients.

The learned and ingenious Translator of Pindar has suggested several striking pleas in his favour, both with respect to the *connection of his thoughts* and the *regularity of his measure*85. To resume on the present occasion any part of what he hath advanced, would be equally useless and improper. As to the first, Ishall only add to this Gentleman's observations, that all the writings of Pindar lxxii which have reached the present times are of the panegyrical kind, in which *remote circumstances* and *distant allusions* are often referred to with great propriety; that sometimes several Odes are inscribed to *the same person*; and that all of them are wrote on subjects too *exactly similar* to afford room for *continued variety of description*, without allowing him frequently to digress. It is obvious that in these circumstances the Poet must have been forcibly prompted to indulge the natural exuberance of his genius, that he might gain materials to fill up his subject, and that he might pay a compliment to his Patron by some digression on the merit of his Ancestors, as well as by an encomium on his personal qualities86. If these considerations do not fully apologize for the excursions of this Great Genius, they render them at least more lxxiiil excusible in him, than the same liberties without an equal inducement can possibly be in any of his imitators.

After all however we must acknowledge, that Pindar has rendered his pieces obscure on many occasions by giving too much scope to a wild imagination; and perhaps the true reason for which he took this liberty was that he *imitated the example of his Predecessors*. He had seen the first Lyric Poets indulging the boldest sallies of Fancy, and applying to particular purposes the Mythology of their country; and as their writings had been held in admiration by succeeding ages, instead of being exposed to the researches of criticism, he was encouraged to proceed in the same course, by the expectation of obtaining a similar reward. From a passage formerly quoted, it would appear that Pindar thought himself peculiarly exempted from conforming to rules of any kind whatever87, and we can suppose this opinion to have proceeded originally from no other foundation than his knowledge of the practice of former authors.

I am sufficiently aware, my Lord, that some readers may object to the preceding theory, that it is probable, if Pindar had been of opinion that Lyric Poetry in his time stood in need of material emendations, the same fertility of invention which enabled him to reach the heighth of excellence in this art, without however altering lxxiv its original principles; that this would have led him likewise to invent new rules, and to supply the deficiencies of his Predecessors. Iwill venture to affirm, that this is the only species of invention, in which we have seldom reason to expect that an Original Genius will attempt to excel.

It hath often been observed, that the earliest productions of a Great Genius are generally the most remarkable for wildness and inequality. Asublime imagination is always reaching at something great and astonishing. Sometimes it seizeth the object of its pursuit, and at others, like a person dizzy with the heighth of his station, it staggers and falls headlong. When the mind of such a person ripens, and his judgment arrives at its full maturity, we have reason to expect that the strain of his competition will be more confident and masterly; but his imagination, cramped by the rules which have been formerly laid down, will be still desirous of *breaking* the *old fetters*, rather than felicitous of *inventing new ones*. Though therefore it must be acknowledged that the same Faculty which is able to invent characters, and to *colour* sentiment may likewise discover the rules and principles of an Art, yet we have no ground to hope that it will often be employed to effectuate a purpose which an Author may consider as in some measure prejudicial.

lxxvl2

To compensate for the blemishes formerly mentioned, the writings of Pindar abound with the most instructive moral sentiments, as well as with the most exquisite beauties of descriptive poetry. The Poet often throws in a reflection of this kind in the most natural manner, as it seems to arise spontaneously from the subject. Thus he prepares the mind to hear of the catastrophe of Tlepolemus by an exclamation perfectly apposite, and appropriated to the occasion.

Αμφι δ' ανδρω-

πων φρεσιν αμπλακιαι

Αναριθμητοι κρεμανται

τουτο δ' αμηκανον εύρειν

Ότι νυν, και εν τελευτα φερτατον ανδρε τυχειν. Pin. Olym. VII.

But wrapt in error is the human mind,

And human bliss is ever insecure;

Know we what fortune yet remains behind?

Know we how long the present shall endure? West.

This method of introducing moral observations adds peculiar dignity and importance to Lyric Poetry, and is likewise happily suited to the Ode, whose diversified composition naturally admits ofit.

I shall only observe further with regard to Pindar, that his character is eminently distinguished by that noble superiority to vulgar opinions, which is the inseparable concomitant of true genius. He appears to have lxxvi had his Zoilus as well as Homer, and to have been equally fallible of the extent and sublimity of his own talents. Thus he compares his enemies to a parcel of crows and magpies pursuing an eagle.

The learned Abbe Fraquier in a short dissertation on the character of Pindar affirms, that one will discover too obvious an imitation of this Poet in those pieces of Horace which are sublime and diversified88. He mentions, as examples of this, his celebrated Odes to Virgil89 and to Galatea90, intended to dissuade them from going to sea; and that in which he so artfully represents to the Roman people the danger and impropriety of removing the seat of the Empire to Troy91. Upon comparing these with the Odes of Pindar, he says that we shall find more strength, more energy, and more sublimity in the works of the Greek, than in those of the Roman Poet92. In the three Odes formerly mentioned, he observes that the digressions never lead us far from the principal subject, and the Poet's imagination appears to be too much confined to one place. On the contrary, Pindar never curbs the lxxvii exuberance of his Genius. He celebrates promiscuously in the same Ode, Gods, Heroes, and persons who have made a shining figure in their age and country, by imitating illustrious examples93.

From the observations made on the manner of Horace in a preceding part of this Essay, it is sufficiently obvious, that his Genius in

Lyric Poetry was principally fitted to excel in the composition of the shorter Ode; and that his imagination was not so equal as that of Pindar to the higher and more perfect species. Of the three Pieces, however, which this Author hath mentioned as imitations of the Greek Poet, we can only admit one to have been compleatly attempted in the manner of this Great Master. It is that which regards the design of removing the imperial seat to Troy. The other two Odes are highly beautiful in their kind; but the subjects are not treated at so much length, nor with that variety of high poetic colouring which characteriseth so eminently the writings of the latter. The Ode to the Roman people is indeed composed in an higher strain, and is full of that enthusiasm which the subject might naturally be supposed to excite in the mind of a Poet, who was animated by the love of his country. Through the whole of this noble performance, the address of the Author, and the emphatical energy with which the sentiments are conveyed, lxxviii deserve to be equally the objects of admiration. The Poem opens with a just and poetical description of the security of Virtue; from which the Poet takes occasion to introduce an artful compliment to Augustus, whom he ranks with Bacchus and Romulus; on the ascent of which last to heaven, Juno expresseth her aversion to the repeopling of Troy. She breaks abruptly into the subject, in a manner expressive of eager solicitude.

— —Ilion, Ilion,

Fatalis incestusque Judex

Et Mulier peregrina vertit

In pulverem.94

Troy,—perjured Troy has felt

The dire effects of her proud tyrant's guilt;—

An Umpire partial and unjust,

And a lewd woman's impious lust,

Lay heavy on her head, and sunk her to the dust. Addison.

She then proceeds in the most artful manner to insinuate, that as the destruction of this city was occasioned by her ingratitude to the Gods, as well as by the particular injury done to her and Minerva, if

Troy should be thrice rebuilt by the hand of Apollo, the Greeks would thrice be permitted to overturn it; and

——ter Uxor

Capta, virum puerosque ploret.95

lxxix

Thrice should her captive dames to Greece return,

And their dead sons, and slaughter'd Husbands mourn. Addison.

The prosperity which she promiseth to the Roman arms is therefore granted, only upon condition that they never think of rebuilding this detested city.

From the preceding short account of this celebrated Ode, it will appear that the transitions are extremely artful, the sentiments noble, and that the whole conduct is happy and judicious. These, if I mistake not, are the distinguishing excellencies of the larger Odes of Horace, in which the Poet's *didactic* genius is remarkably conspicuous. Perhaps however, your Lordship, like the French Critic, is at a loss to find in all this, the energy, the vehemence, the exuberance of Pindar. Horace himself was perfectly sensible of the superior excellence of the Greek Poet, and never rises to truer sublimity than when he is drawing his character. The following image is great, and appropriated to the subject.

Monte decurrens velut amnis, imbres

Quem super notas aluere ripas

Fervet, immensusque *ruit* profundo

Pindarus ore.96

Pindar like some fierce torrent swoln with show'rs,

Or sudden Cataracts of melting Snow,

Which from the Alps its headlong Deluge pours,

And foams, and thunders o'er the Vales below,

lxxx

With desultory fury borne along,

Rolls his impetuous, vast, unfathomable song. West.

I know not, my Lord, how it happens, that we generally find our-selves more highly pleased with excess and inequality in poetic composition, than with the serene, the placid, and the regular pro-gression of a corrected imagination. Is it because the mind is satiat-ed with uniformity of any kind, and that remarkable blemishes, like a few barren fields interspersed in a landschape give additional lustre to the more cultivated scenery? Or does it proceed from a propensity in human nature to be pleased, when we observe a great Genius sometimes *sinking as far below the common level*, as at others, he is capable of *rising above it*? Iconfess, that I am inclined to deduce this feeling more frequently from the *former* than from the *latter* of these causes; though I am afraid that the warmest *benevolence* will hardly prevail upon your Lordship not to attribute it in some in-stances to *a mixture of both*.

Whatever may be in this, it is certain that the Odes of Horace, in which he has professedly imitated Pindar, are much more correct and faultless than these of his Master. It would, perhaps, be saying too much, to affirm with some Critics, that the judgment of the Ro-man Poet was superior to that of his Rival; but it is obvious, that the operation of this Faculty is more remarkable in lxxxim his writings, because his imagination was more ductile and pliable. —Upon the whole, therefore, we shall not do injustice to these two great men, if we assign to their works the same degree of comparative excellence, which the Italians ascribe to the pieces of Dominichino and Guido. The former was a *great* but an *unequal Genius;* while the more cor-rected performances of the latter were *animated by the Graces*, and *touched by the pencil of Elegance*97.

I am afraid, that your Lordship is now thinking it high time to bring the whole of this detail to a period.— — Upon reviewing the observations made on the Lyric Poetry of the Ancients through the preceding part of this Essay, lxxxii you will find that the subject has been considered under the three following heads. In the first part I have attempted to lay before your Lordship, the state of Lyric Poet-ry in the earliest ages, as it appears from what we can collect either of the character of the writings of Amphion, Linus, Orpheus, Mu-seus, and Hesiod. In the course of this enquiry I have had occasion to assign the causes, whose concurrence rendered this branch of the poetic Art less perfect at its first introduction than any of the other species. — Upon advancing a little further, a richer and more diversified prospect opened to the imagination. In *the first dawn* of this more enlightened period, we meet with the names of Alcaeus and Sappho, who, without altering *the original character* of the Ode, made a considerable change on the *subjects* to which it was appropriated; and in *the full meridian* of Science, we find this second form of Lyric Poetry brought to its highest perfection in the writings of Horace. — Some remarks on the nature of those beauties which are peculiarly characteristic of the *higher species* of the Ode, and on the part which Imagination particularly claims in its composition, led me to mention, a few rules, the exact observation of which will, perhaps, contribute to render this species of poetry more correct and regular, without retrenching any part of its *discriminating* beauties, and without straitning too much the Genius of the Poet. With this view I lxxxiiim2 have endeavoured to characterize impartially the pindaric manner, by pointing out *its excellencies*, by enumerating *its defects*, and by enquiring from what particular causes the latter are to be deduced.

I consider it, my Lord, as a circumstance particularly agreeable on the present occasion, that the Persons who are most capable to observe the *defects* of an Author, are likewise commonly the readiest to *excuse them*. Little minds, like the fly on the Edifice, will find many inequalities in *particular members* of a work, which an enlarged understanding either overlooks as insignificant, or contemplates as *the mark of human imperfection*. Iam, however, far from intending to insinuate, that feelings of this nature will prevail on your Lordship to consider real blemishes merely as the effects of an inadvertency, which is excusable in proportion to the intricacy of a subject. Ihave been induced to throw together the preceding remarks, with an intention to rescue Lyric Poetry from the contempt in which it has been unjustly held by Authors of unquestioned penetration, to prove that it is naturally susceptible of the *highest poetic beauty*; and that under proper regulations, it may be made subservient to purposes as beneficial as any other branch of the Art. These facts will indeed be sufficiently obvious to persons unacquainted with the Ancients, by perusing the works of eminent *Poets* of the present age, whose names it lxxxiv would be superfluous to mention. Idismiss this attempt, and the pieces which accompany it, to the judgment of the public, with that timidity and diffidence which the review of so many great names, and the sense of Inexperience are fitted to inspire. Whatever may be the fate of either, Ishall remember, with pleasure, that they have afforded me an opportunity of testifying that high and respectful esteem, with which I have the Honour tobe,

MY LORD,

YOUR LORDSHIP's

MOST OBLIGED,

AND MOST OBEDIENT SERVANT,

J. OGILVIE.

1. Neque ipsa Ratio (says the elegant and sensible Quintilian speaking of Eloquence) tam nos juvaret, nisi quæ concepissemus mente, promere etiam loquendo possemus, — ita, ut non modo orare, sed quod Pericli contigit fulgerare, ac tonare videamur. Institut. Orat. Lib. XI. c.16.

2. This is the manner which Quintilian appropriates particularly to young persons. — In juvenibus etiam uberiora paulo & pene periclitantia feruntur. At in iisdem siccum, & contractum dicendi propositum plerunque affectatione ipsa severitatis invisum est: quando etiam morum senilis autoritas immatura in adolescentibus creditur. Lib. II. c.1.

3.Εοικασι δε γεννησαι μεν ὁλως την Ποιητικην, αιτιαι δυο και αυται φυσικαι.Το μιμεισθαι συμφυτον τοις ανθρωποις, &c. Και Ἁρμονια και ρυθμος εξ αρχης οἱ πεφυκοτες προς αυτα μαλιστα κατα μικρον προαγοντες εγεινησαν την Ποιησιν·C Arist. Poet. c.4.

4. The Reader of curiosity may see this subject particularly discussed in Dacier's Remarks on the Poeticks of Aristotle, c.4.

5.Ἁ γαρ αυτα λυπηρως ὁρωμεν, τουτων τας εικωνας τας μαλιστα ηκριβωμενας, χαιρομεν θεωρουντες, οἱτινες θηρεων τε μορφας των αγριοτατων και νεκρων,C &c. Poet. c.4.

6.Τα γαρ μετρα ὁτι μοιρον των ρυθμων εστι, φανερον.C Ub. sup.

7.Ρυθμον μεν και σχηματα μελους χωρις λογους ψιλους εις μετρα τιθεντες. The persons who do this, he compares to Musicians. Μελος δε αυ και ρυθμους ανευ ρηματων ψιλη κιθαριξει τε και αυλησει προσχρωμενοι.D Plat. de Legib. Lib.XI.

8. Plat. Io.

9. Nec prima illa post secula per ætates sane complures alio Lyrici spectarunt, quam ut Deorum laudes ac decora, aut virorum fortium res preclare gestas Hymnis ac Pæanibus, ad templa & aras complecterentur;—ut ad emulationem captos admiratione mortales invitarent. Strad. Prolus. 4 Poet.

10. Hor. de Art. Poet.

11. Id. ibid.

12. Toute Poesie est une imitation. La Poesie Bucolique a pour but d'imiter ce qui a passe et ce qui ce dit entre les Bergers. Mem. de Lit. V.III. p.158.

13. Elle ne doit pas s'en tenir a la simple representation du vrai reel, qui rarement seroit agreable; elle doit s'elever jusqu'au *vrai ideal*, qui tend' a embellir le vrai, tel qu'il est dans la nature, et qui produit dans la Poesie comme dans la Peinture, le derniere point de perfeftion, &c. Mem. de Lit. ub. sup.

14. Thucyd. Lib. I.

15. Id. ibid.

16. Authors are not agreed as to the Persons who introduced into Greece the principles of philosophy. Tatian will have it that the Greek Philosophy came originally from Ægypt. Orat. con. Graec. While Laertius (who certainly might have been better informed) will allow Foreigners to have had no share in it. He ascribes its origin to Linus, and says expressly, Αφ' Ἑλληνων ηρξε φιλοσοφια ἡς και αυτο το ονομα την Βαρβαρον απεστραπτε προσηγοριαν. Laer. in Prœm.

17. This account of the subjects on which Linus wrote, suggests a further prejudice in favour of Laertius's opinion as to the origin of Greek Philosophy. He has preserved the first line of his Poem.

Ην ποτε χρονος ούτος εν ώ άμα παντ' επεφυκει. Id. ibid.

18. Herod. Lib. I. c. 49.

19. Univ. Hist. Vol. VI. p. 221.

20. Οἱ μεν γαρ σεμνοτεροι τας καλας εμιμουντο πραξεις και τας των τοιουτων τυχας· οἱ δε ευτελεστεροι τας των φαυλων πρωτον ψογους ποιουντες, ὡσπερ έτεροι ΥΜΝΟΥΣ και ΕΓΚΩΜΙΑ. Arist. Poet. c.4.

21. Orph. Argonaut.

22. Εγω δε ει τον περι θεων εξαγορευσαντα τοιαυτα· χρη φιλοσοφον καλειν ουκ οιδα τινα δει προσαγορευιν τον το ανθρωπειον παθος αφειδουντο τοις θεοις προστριψαι, και τα σπασιως ὑπο τοιων ανθρωπων αισχρουργουμενα, και τω ταυτης φωνης οργανω. Laer. ub. sup.

23. Hor. de Art. Poet.

24. The beautiful story of Hero and Leander, which was written by a person of his name, is thought to have been the work of a Grammarian who lived about the 5th century: a conjecture support-ed by very probable evidence. See Kenneth's life of Museus, p.10.

25. Diogen. Laert. ub. sup.

26. Diogen. Laert. ub. sup.

27. Æneid. Lib. 6.

28. It may not be amiss here to give the reader some idea of the structure of the Ancient lyre, whose music is said to have produced such wonderful effects. This instrument was composed of an hollow frame, over which several strings were thrown, probably in some such manner as we see them in an harp, or a dulcimer. They did not so much resemble the viol, as the neck of that instrument gives it peculiar advantages, of which the Ancients seem to have been wholly ignorant. The Musician stood with a short bow in his right hand, and a couple of small thimbles upon the fingers of his left: with these he held one end of the string, from which an acute sound

was to be drawn, and then struck it immediately with the bow. In the other parts he swept over every string alternately, and allowed each of them to have its full sound. This practice became unnecessary afterwards, when the instrument was improved by the addition of new strings, to which the sounds corresponded. Horace tells us, that in his time the lyre had seven strings, and that it was much more musical than it had been originally. Addressing himself to Mercury, he says

— —Te docilis magistro.

Movit Amphion lapides canendo:

Tuque Testudo, resonare septem

Callida nervis;

Nec loquax olim, neque grata *&c.*
Carm. Lib. III. Od. 11.

For a further account of this instrument, we shall refer the reader to Quintilian's Institutions. Lib. XII. c.10.

29. Particularly Orpheus and Museus. Lucian says in the general. Τελετην αρχαιαν ουδεμιαν εστιν εύρειν ανου ορχησεως. Lib. de Salt.

30. This allegorical learning was so much in use among the Ægyptians, that the Disciples of a Philosopher were bound by an oath. Εν ὑποκρυφοις ταυτα εχειν· και τοις απαιδευτοις και αμνητοις μη μεταδεδιναι. Vid. Seld. de Diis Syr.

31.

— — —— —— —— Ἡσιν αοιδη

Μεμβλεται, εν στηθεσσιν ακηδεα θυμον εχουσαις

Τυτθον απ᾽ ακροτατης κορυφης νιφεντος Ολυμπου.

Ενθα σφιν λιπαροι τε χοροι, και δωματα καλα.Ε
Theog. a lin. 61.

32.

Ὡς εφασαν Ηουραι Μεγαλου Διος αρτιεπειαι·

Και μοι σκεπτρον εδον, δαφνης εριθελεος οζον

Δρεψασθαι θηητον· επενευσαν δε μοι αυδην &c.
Theogon. l. 30.

33. Orph. Hym. in Apollon. Rhod.

34. Of this, History furnisheth many examples. When one man made an eminent figure in any profession, the actions of other persons who had the same name were ascribed to him; and it was perhaps partly for this reason that we find different cities contending for the honour of giving birth to men of Genius, or eminence. Callimachus in his Hymn to Jupiter makes an artful use of this circumstance.

Εν δοιη μαλα θυμος· επει γενος αμφεριστον.

Ζευ σε μεν Ἰ᾽ δαιοισιν εν ουρεσι φασι γενεσθαι

Ζευ σε δ᾽ εν Αρκαδιη· ποτεροι Πατερ εψευσαντο

Κρητες αει ψευσται· και γαρ ταφον, ὡ ανα σειο

Κρητες ετεκτηναντο· συ δ᾽ ου θανες· εσσι γαρ αιει.
Callim. p. 4.

35. Thus Theocritus.

Ὑμνεομες Ληδας. Τε και αιγιοχω Διος Ὑιω,

Καστορα και φοβερον Πολυδευκεα πυξ ερεθιζεν

Ὑμνεομες και Δις, και το Τριτον.

36. Anac. Carm. p. 35.

37. Anac. p. 87.

38. This appears remarkably in that piece, where he gives so ingenuous a character of himself.

Ὁν μοι μελει Γυγου

Του Σαρδεων Ανακτος, &c.

Το σημερον μελει μοι.
p.28.

39. The reader will find a striking example of this beauty, in the Ode addressed to a swallow, where he runs a comparison betwixt the liberty of that bird and his own bondage.

Συ μεν φιλη χελιδων, &c. p.60.

40. Thus Horace represents her

Æoliis fidibus quærentem

Sappho puellis de popularibus.
Lib. II. Od.13.

41.Θεου ἡ Σαπφω τα συμβαινοντα ταις ερωτικαις μανιαις παθηματα εκ των παρεπομενων, και εκ της αληθειας, αυτης ἑκαστοτε λαμβανει, &c. De Lub. c.10.

42. Longinus speaks with transport of this beautiful fragment of antiquity. Ου θαυμαζεις ὡς ὑπ᾽ αυτο την ψυχην το σωμα τας ακοας την γλωσσαν τας οψεις την χροαν, πανθ᾽ ὡς αλλοτρια διοιχομενοι επιζητει.Και καθ᾽ ὑπεναντιωσεις ἁμα ψυχεται, καιεται, αλογιστει, φρονει—ἱνα μη εν τι περι αυτην παθος φαινεται, παθων δε ΣΥΝΟΔΟΣ. De. Lub. c.10.

43.

Te sonantem plenius aureo

Alcæe plectro, dura navis,

Dura fugæ mala, dura belli.

Utrumque sacro digna silentio

Mirantur Utmbræ dicere.
— —*Hor. ub. sup.*

44.

Liberum & Musas, Veneremque & illi

Semper hærentem puerum canebat,

Et Lycum nigris oculis nigroque

Crine decorum.
Carm. Lib. I. Od.32.

45. Carm. Lib. I. Od. 13.

46. Carm. Lib. II. Od. 9.

47. Id. Lib. III. Od. 4.

48. Carm. Lib. II. Od. 6.

49. Polycrates, Tyrant of Samos.

50. Hor. de Art. Poet.

51. Id. ibid.

52. Aristotle expressly mentions this circumstance, when he explains the Origin of the Drama. Παραφανεισας δε της Τραγωδιας και Κωμωδιας, οἱ εφ' ἑκατερον τη ποιησεν ἁρμωντες κατα την οικειαν φυσιν οἱ μεν αντι των Ιαμβων, Κωμωδοποιοι εγενοντο· οἱ δε αντι των Επων τραγωδιδασκαλοι, δια τω μειζω και ενεμοτερα τα σχηματα ειναι ταυτα εκεινων.F Arist. Poet. c.4.

53. Boil. Art. Poet.

54. Les grands Orateurs n'emploient que des expressions riches capables de faire valoir leurs raisons. Ils tachent d'eblouir les yeux, et l'esprit, et pour ce sujet ils ne combattent qu'avec des armes brillantes. Lam. Rhet. Liv. IV. c.13.

55. Hor. de Arte Poet.

56. Una cuique proposita lex, suus decor est. Habet tamen omnis Eloquentia aliquid commune. Quintil. Instit. Lib.X c.II.

57. In the Epopee we judge of the Genius of the Poet, by the variety and excellence of those materials with which Imagination enricheth his subject. His Judgment appears in the disposition of particular images, and in the general relation which every subordinate part bears to the principal action of the Poem. Thus it is the business of this Faculty, as an ingenious Critic says, "Considerer comme un corps qui no devoit pas avoir des membres de natures differentes, et independens les uns des autres." Bossu du Poem. Epiq. Liv.II. ch.2. It is true indeed, that Tragedy is rather an address to the passions than to the imagination of mankind. To the latter however we must refer all those finer strokes of poetic painting, which actuate so forcibly the affections and the heart. We may, in short, easily conceive the importance of a warm imagination to the Dramatic Poet, by reflecting upon the coldness and indifference with which we peruse those pieces, which are not enlivened by the sallies of this Faculty when it is properly corrected. Though we must acknowledge that Passion seldom adopts the images of description, yet it must be owned at the same time, that neither can a person who wants imag-

ination feel with sensibility the impulse of the Passions. A Poet may even merit a great encomium who excels in painting the effects, and in copying the language of Passion, though the Disposition of his work may be otherwise irregular and faulty. Thus Aristotle says of a celebrated dramatic Poet, Και Ὁ Ευριπιδης ει και τα αλλα μη ευ οικονομει, αλλα ΤΡΑΓΙΚΩΤΑΤΟΣ γε των Ποιητων φαινεται. De Poet. c. 13. Upon the whole therefore, Didactic or Ethical Poetry is the only species in which Imagination acts but a secondary part, because it is unquestionably the business of reason to fix upon the most forcible arguments, as well as to throw them into the happiest disposition. We have seen however, in some late performances, what superior advantages this branch of the Art receives from a just and proper infusion of the poetic idioms.

58. For this reason, says an ingenious and learned Critic, L'Ode monte dans les Cieux, pour y empronter ses images et ses comparaisons du tonnerre, des astres, et des Dieux memes, &c. Reflex. Crit. Vol. I. Sect.33.

59.Εγω δε οιδα μεν ὡς αἱ ὑπερβολαι μεγεθους φυσαι ἡκιστα καθαραι.Το γαρ εν παντα ακριβες, κινδυνος σμικροτητος· εν δε τοις μεγεθεσιν ὡσπερ εν τοις αγαν πλουτοις, ειναι τε χρη και παραλιγωρουμενον.Μη ποτε ηδε τουτο και αναγκαιουσιν, το τας μεν ταπεινας και μεσας φυσεις δια το μηδαμη παρακινδυνευειν μηδε εφιεσθαι των ακρων, αδαμαρτητου ὡς επι το πολυ και ασφαλεστερας διαφερειν. Longin. de Sublim. Sect.33.

60. De Sublim. Sect. 32.

61. The reader will observe, that Admiration through the whole of this part of the Essay is taken in the largest sense, as including a considerable degree of wonder, which is however a distinct feeling. The former is excited principally by the sublime; the latter by the new and uncommon. These feelings are united, when a subject of moderate dignity is treated in a sublime manner. See the Essay, p.47,48.

62. Raphael is said to have stolen the expression of this figure from Michael Angelo, who was at work on the same subject in another part of the Vatican. We are indebted for this curious anecdote to the ingenious Abbe du Bos. See his Reflex. Crit. sur la Poes. et la Peint. Vol.II.

63. Callim. Hymn. in Jov. a lin.68. G

64. Pind. Pyth. I.

65. Iliad. Lib. VIII. H

66. This is one of the most artful and best conducted of Pindar's Odes. The introduction is abrupt and spirited, and the Heroe of the Poem is shown to great advantage.

Αναξιφορμιγγες ὑμνοι

τινα θεον, τιν᾽ ἠροα,

τινα δ᾽ ανδρα κελαδησομεν;

ητοι πισα μεν Διος·

Ολυμπιαδα δ᾽ εστα-

σεν Ηρακλεης, &c.

Θηρωνα δε τετραοριας

ἑνεκα νεκαφορου

γεγωνητεον, οπε &c.
Pind. Olym. 2da.

67. The reader will meet with many examples of this liberty in the Iliad, some of which Mr. Pope has judiciously selected in the notes of his translation. Milton, in the same spirit, compares Satan lying on the lake of fire, to a Leviathan slumbering on the coast of Norway; and immediately digressing from the strict points of connection, he adds, "that the mariners often mistake him for an island, and cast anchor on his side." Par. Lost, B.II. In this illustration it is obvious, that though the Poet deviates from close imitation, yet he still keeps in view the general end of his subject, which is to exhibit a picture of the fallen Arch angel. See Par. Lost, B.I.

68. The reader may consider, as an example, of the following verses of the Ode of Sophocles to the Sun.

Πολλα γαρ ὡστ᾽ ακαμαντος

η Νωτου η Βορεα τις

κυματα ευρει ποντω

βαντ' επιοντα τ' ιδοι

ούτο δε τον καδμογενη

τρεφει· το δ' αυξει βιοτου

πολυπονον ώστε πελαγος

κρητιον.
Soph. Trachin.

69. Of this the reader will find a noble instance in Pindar's first Pythian Ode, where he employs from the verse beginning ναυσιφορηταις δ' αδρασεα,I &c. to the end of the stanza, one of the happiest and most natural illustrations that is to be met with either in the works of Pindar, or in those of any Poet whatever. The abrupt address to Phœbus, when he applies the metaphor, is peculiarly beautiful.

70. Hor. Epist. Lib. II. Epist.1.

71. Pin. Pyth. Ode X.

72. Letter I. p.xxxiii.

73. Pin. Nem. Ode XI.

74. Id. Olym. Ode VII.

75. Hor. de Art. Poet.

76. Pind. Pyth. Ode XI.

77. Thus the reader, who would pay little regard to the person who should forbid him to trust the world too much, will yet be struck with this simple admonition, when it appears in the work of a genius.

Lean not on earth, 'twill pierce thee to the heart;

A broken reed at best, but oft' a spear,

On its sharp point Peace bleeds, and Hope expires. Night Thoughts.

78. Thus Xenophon, the simplest and most perspicuous of Historians, has borrowed many noble images from Homer; and Plato is often indebted to this Poet, whom yet he banished from his Commonwealth. Cicero in his most serious pieces studies the *diction*, and

copies the *manner* of the Greek Philosopher; and it evidently appears, that Thucydides has taken many a *glowing Metaphor* from the Odes of Pindar. We might produce many examples of this from their writings, if these would not swell this note to too great a length. The reader of taste may see this subject fully discussed in Mr. Gedde's ingenious Essay on the Composition of the Ancients.

79.Δει δε τους μυθους συνισταναι, και τη λεξει συναπεργαζεσθαι οντι μαλιστα προς ομματων τεθεμενον.Οὑτο γαρ αν εναργεστατα ὁρων ὡσπερ παρ' αυτοις γιγνομενος τοις πραττομενοις, εὑρισκοι το πρεπον, και ἡκιστα αν λανθανοιτο τα ὑπεναντια.Κ Arist. Poet. c.17.

80. Thus Cicero tells us. Nec est majus in dicendo, quam ut Orator sic moveatur, ut impetu quodam animi, & perturbatione magis quam concilio regatur. Plura enim multo homines judicant odio, & amore, & cupiditate, &c. quam veritate & præscripto. De Orat. Lib. II. c.42.

81. Volt. Siec. Louis XIV. c. 21.

82. Cebet. Tab.

83. Upon the principle established here, we may account in some measure for Voltaire's apparently paradoxical assertion, with regard to the comparative merit of Homer and Tasso. The Italian (says that spirited writer) has more conduct, variety and justness than the Greek. Admitting the truth of this reflection, we might still reply, that the principal merit of the Iliad, considered as the production of Genius, lies in the grandeur of the sentiments, the beauty and sublimity of the illustrations, and the *original* strokes which are wrought into the description of the *principal Actors*. In all these respects we may venture to affirm, that Homer remains without a superior among Authors unaided by Inspiration; and the reader must be left to judge whether or not it is from these criterions that we estimate the Genius of a Poet. Our Author proceeds upon the same principles to compare the Orlando Furioso with the Odyssey, and give a preference to the former. The merit of these works may be ascertained in some measure, by the rules we have already established. We need only to add further on this head, that among many beauties we meet with examples of the turgid and bombast in the work of Ariosto; from which that of the Greek Poet is wholly free. The two first lines of his Poem,

Le Donne, e Cavalieri, l'arme, gli amore,

Le Cortesie l'audaci impresi io canto.

if they do not put one in mind of the Cyclic Writer mentioned by Horace, who begins his Poem with

Fortunam Priami cantabo, & nobile bellum.

yet are of a very different strain from those which introduce the Odyssey,

Ανδρα μοι ενεπε Μουσα πολυτροπον, ὅς μαλα πολλα

Πλαγκθη &c.

I cannot help thinking that the whole of this introduction is remarkably simple and unornamented, though a very judicious and ingenious Critic seems to be of a contrary opinion.

84. Hab. ch. iii. v. 3.

85. Mr. West. See the Preface and Notes of his Translation.

86. It is generally to be supposed, that a Poet in a panegyrical address to his Patron will select with solicitude every circumstance in his character and actions which excite approbation, in order to render his encomium as perfect and compleat as possible. When therefore he is unexpectedly engaged to retouch a subject which he had formerly discussed, we ought to expect, either that he will fix upon *new points of panegyric*, which is always a matter of the greatest difficulty; or we must indulge him in the liberty of calling in *adventitious assistance*, when he is deprived of other materials. This appears on many occasions to have been the case of Pindar. No less than four of his Odes are inscribed to Hiero King of Syracuse, all on account of his victories in the Games of Greece. Two Odes immediately following the first to Hiero are addressed to Theron King of Agrigentum; Psaumis of Camarina is celebrated in the 4th and 5th Olympic; and the 9th and 10th are filled with the praises of Agesidamus the Locrian. Every reader must make *great allowances* for a Poet, who was so often obliged to retouch and to *diversify* subjects of one kind.

87. Vide supra, p. 57.

88. Ce son des tableaux d'un Eleve habile, ou l'on reconnoit la maniere du Maitre, bien qu' on n'y retrouve pas a beaucoup près tout son genie. Mem. de Liter. Tom. III. p.49.

89. Car. Lib. I. Od. 3.

90. Id. Lib. III. Od. 27.

91. Carm. Lib. III. Ode 3.

92. Il est aise d'en marquer la difference sans parler de celle du stile qui dans Pindare a toujours plus de force, plus d'energie, & plus de noblesse que dans Horace, &c. Mem. de Lit. ubi supra.

93. Id. ibid.

94. Car. Lib. III. Od. 3.

95. Id. ibid.

96. Car. Lib. IV. Od. 2.

97. The Reader will observe, that nothing has been said in this Essay on the regularity of the measure of Pindar's Odes. This subject is treated so fully in the preface of Mr. West's Translation, that we need only here to refer the curious to his remarks. The Ancient Odes are always to be considered as songs which were set to musick, and whose recital was generally accompanied with dancing. If we may be permitted to form an idea of this music, from the nature and composition of the Ode, it must have been a matter of great difficulty to excel in it, as it is certain that poems which abound with sentiments are more proper to be set to music, than those which are ornamented with imagery. These sister-arts usually keep pace with each other, either in their improvement or decay. Ne ci dobbiamo (says an ingenious Foreigner, speaking of the modern Italian music) maravigliare, ce corrotta la Poesia, s'e anche corrotta la musica; perche come nella ragior poetica accennammo, tutte le arti imitative hanno una idea commune, dalla cui alterazione si alterano tutte, eparticolarmenti la musica dall alterazion del la poesia si cangia come dal corpo l'ombra. Onde corrotta la poesia da e soverchi ornamenti e dalla copia delle figure, ha communicato anche il suo morbo alla musica, ormai tanto sfigurata, che ha perduta quasi la natural est pressione. Gavina della Traged. p.70.B

Supplementary Notes
(*added by transcriber*)

Handwriting

The facsimile of the title page includes two handwritten lines between "Lord Deskfoord" and the author's name:

> **The Right Honourable J A M E S Lord DESKFOORD.**
>
> *The last Earl of Findlater who died 1812 without ifsue*
> *Title claimed by Sir Wm Ogilvie Bart of Carnousie who died Feb 20th 1861*
>
> **By JOHN OGILVIE, A.M.**

The last Earl of Findlater who died 1812 without ifsue

Title claimed by Sir Wm Ogilvie Bart of Carnousie, who died Feb 20^th^1861

The two lines were probably written at different times: the first uses long "s" while the second had to have been written in or after 1861. The underlined year "1812" is an error for 1811 (October). The William Ogilvie (more often spelled Ogilvy) of the second line was born in 1810, so his claim to the title cannot have been immediate. He does not appear to have been related to the book's author.

Italian

The quotation from Gravina (misspelled Gavina), *Della Tragedia*, is given exactly as printed in note 97, including clear errors. The passage appears in the 1819 *Opere Scelte* (Selected Works) as:

Né ci dobbiamo maravigliare, se corrotta la poesia, si è anche corrotta la musica: perché, come nella Ragion Poetica accennammo, tutte le arti imitative hanno una idea comune, dalla cui alterazione si alterano tutte; eparticolarmente la musica dall' alterazion della poesia si cangia, come dal corpo l'ombra. Onde corrotta la poesia dai soverchi ornamenti e dalla copia delle figure, ha comunicato il suo morbo anche alla musica, ormai tanto figurata, che ha perduta quasi la natural espressione.

Greek

The printed Greek used no diacritics, except for the one word ὅς (including accent) in the Odyssey quotation. All other rough-breathing marks have been added by the transcriber. Line breaks in verse citations are as in the original.

The errors are unusual. Instead of confusing similar letters such as υ and ν, or garbling diacritics, the Greek passages read as if they were learned orally, and written down from memory. Substitutions of ο for ω and ι for ε are especially common. The more significant differences between Ogilvie's text and "standard" readings are given here.

Aristotle, *Poetics* 1448b (in notes 3, 5, 6 as "c. 4"):

Και Ἁρμονια και ρυθμος εξ αρχης
or: τῆς ἁρμονίας καὶ τοῦ ῥυθμοῦ ... ἐξ ἀρχῆς
οίτινες θηρεων τε μορφας των αγριοτατων και νεκρων
or: οἶον θηρίων τε μορφὰς τῶν ἀτιμοτάτων καὶ νεκρῶν
Τα γαρ μετρα ότι μοιρον των ρυθμων ...
or: τὰ γὰρ μέτρα ὅτι μόρια τῶν ῥυθμῶν ...

Plato, *Leges* 669de (in note 7 as "Lib. XI"):

Μελος δε αυ και ρυθμους ανευ ρημα<u>των</u>
or: μέλος δ' αὖ καὶ ῥυθμὸν ἄνευ ῥημάτων

Hesiod, *Theogony* 31 (in note 31 as l. 63):

Δρεψασθαι θηητον· επενευσαν δε μοι αυδην
or: δρέψασαι, θηητόν· ἐνέπνευσαν δέ μοι αὐδὴν

Aristotle, *Poetics* 1449a (in note 52 as "c. 4"):

... οἱ δε αντι των Επων τραγωδιδασκαλοι, δια τω μειζω και ενεμοτερα τα σχηματα ειναι ...

or: ... οἱ δὲ ἀντὶ τῶν ἐπῶν τραγῳδοδιδάσκαλοι, διὰ τὸ μείζω καὶ ἐντιμότερα τὰ σχήματα εἶναι ...

Callimachus I. 68-69 (body text and note 63):

Θηκαο δ' οιωνον μεγ' ὑπειροχον αγγελεωτην,

Σων τεραων· ἁτ' εμοισι φιλοις ενδεξια φαινοις

or:

θήκαο δ' οἰωνῶν μέγ' ὑπείροχον ἀγγελιώτην

σῶν τεράων· ἅ τ' ἐμοῖσι φίλοις ἐνδέξια φαίνοι

Iliad VIII. 438-443 (body text and note 65):

Ζευς δε Πατηρ ιδηθεν ευτροχον άρμα και ίππους

Ολυμπονδ' εδιωκε, θεων δ' εξεκετο θωκους.

Τω δε και ίππους μεν λυσε κλυτος Εννοσιγαιος

Άρματα δ' αμβρωμοισι τιθει, κατα λιτα πετασσας.

Αυτος δε χρυσειον επι θρωνον ευρυοπα Ζευς

Έζετο, τω δε ύπο ποσσι μεγας πελεμιζετ' Ολυμπος.

or:

Ζεὺς δὲ πατὴρ Ἴδηθεν εὔτροχον ἅρμα καὶ ἵππους

Οὔλυμπον δὲ δίωκε, θεῶν δ' ἐξίκετο θώκους.

τῷ δὲ καὶ ἵππους μὲν λῦσε κλυτὸς ἐννοσίγαιος,

ἅρματα δ' ἅμ βωμοῖσι τίθει κατὰ λῖτα πετάσσας:

αὐτὸς δὲ χρύσειον ἐπὶ θρόνον εὐρύοπα Ζεὺς

ἕζετο, τῷ δ' ὑπὸ ποσσὶ μέγας πελεμίζετ' Ὄλυμπος.

Pindar, *Pythian* **I. 33** (note 69):

ναυσιφορηταις δ' αδρασεα
or: ναυσιφορήτοις δ' ἀνδράσι

Aristotle, *Poetics* **1455a** (in note 79 as "c. 17"):

Δει δε τους μυθους συνισταναι, και τη λεξει συναπεργαζεσθαι οντι μαλιστα προς ομματων τεθεμενον. Ούτο γαρ αν' εναργεστατα όρων ώσπερ παρ αυτοις γιγνομενος τοις πραττομενοις, εύρισκοι το πρεπον, και ήκιστα αν' λανθανοιτο τα ύπεναντια.

or: δεῖ δὲ τοὺς μύθους συνιστάναι καὶ τῇ λέξει συναπεργάζεσθαι ὅτι μάλιστα πρὸ ὀμμάτων τιθέμενον: οὕτω γὰρ ἂν ἐναργέστατα [ὁ] ὁρῶν ὥσπερ παρ' αὐτοῖς γιγνόμενος τοῖς πραττομένοις εὑρίσκοι τὸ πρέπον καὶ ἥκιστα ἂν λανθάνοι [τὸ] τὰ ὑπεναντία.